#98

BEST of both WORLDS #4

Cover Design by Kari March Designs

Cover Photographer Cadwallader Photography

Editing by Happily Editing Anns

www.authoremilysilver.com

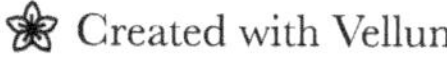 Created with Vellum

BEST OF BOTH WORLDS

A Colorado Black Diamonds Novel

EMILY SILVER

Family Tree

For anyone that needs a family tree of the Denver Mountain Lions & Colorado Black Diamonds, this gives you everything you need to know. Colin & Peyton don't have any kids -- just lots of dogs.

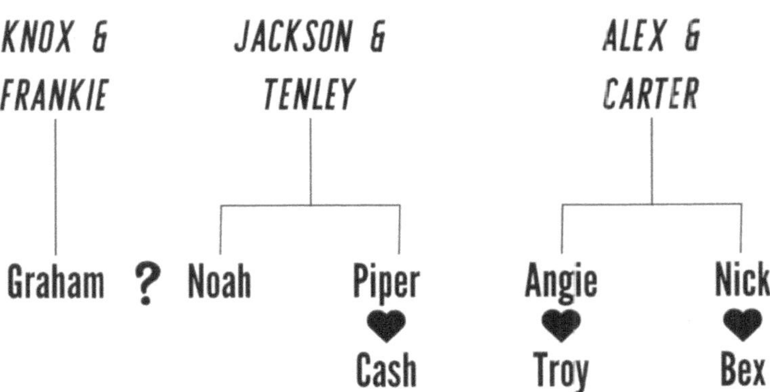

Prologue

NOAH

This fucking sucks.

Eight years in the league, one bad injury, and now I've been dumped without ceremony. It's not like it's my fault that my knee wouldn't cooperate. Instead of heading into the playoffs with the Black Diamonds, I'm standing outside the boards watching my new team play.

The Nashville Knights.

Arguably the worst team in the league.

Seriously. This fucking sucks.

And I'm not even in Nashville yet. I had enough time to pack a bag in Denver, fly to San Jose for the game tonight, and then I'll travel with the team back to Nashville after a short stretch of away games.

I can't even learn the ice here because it's not my home ice. Not like I'd get any actual playing time tonight since it's my first day with the team.

I twist the stick currently in my hand, trying to ward off all the bad feelings that are threatening to overwhelm me.

"Noah. Good to have you here." Coach Andrews claps me on the shoulder as I turn to face him.

He's one of the younger coaches in the league, brought in this year to help the flailing Knights try to find the greatness that I've been used to my entire career. With a shaved head and thick Coke-bottle glasses, he is the furthest thing you'd expect from a head coach.

But after playing in the league for a few years, he started coaching in college and made quite the name for himself.

Maybe he'll help turn this team around.

I guess, *my team* around. That is going to take a while to wrap my head around.

"Thanks, Coach." I stick out my hand for him to shake.

"Nice to not be the only new guy around here."

"Hopefully we'll both adjust quickly," I tell him.

"Then what do you say we get started? You won't be starting against San Jose tonight, but we thought it'd be good to get your skates under you today."

"Sounds good."

Even though I resent him the tiniest bit—well, not him, but the team—I'm ready to get out on the ice. It's the one place I feel most comfortable. Even if I might be out of my element with a brand-new team.

It feels like the first day of school as I follow Coach Andrews out onto the ice. He blows the whistle to halt practice and brings everyone's attention to where we're standing.

"Alright, men. I'd like to introduce your newest teammate, Noah Fields. We're lucky to have a player of his caliber join us, so make sure you all make him feel welcome."

A few people call out in greeting as my eyes flit across

all of them. I have no idea how these guys will react to me. No idea how they play.

Are they selfish with the puck? Are they willing to learn from a more seasoned player? Are we going to continue to be at the bottom of the league every year?

And that's when I see him.

Graham fucking Fisher.

The entire reason I'm here to start with. He's standing back with a few of my new teammates, all guys I recognize from playing against them over the years. Even though we only see each other in passing here and there, faces have become familiar. A quick hello sometimes after games.

Marcus Evans.

Jasper Hayes.

Bode Adams.

Dax Fletcher.

All good guys. Except Fisher.

With one hit, he changed my entire playing career. I didn't miss the way he looked at me when I went down. I couldn't get a read on his face, but I hated the look there. Like he wished he hit me harder.

Asshole.

Dark brown eyes are staring at me under the shield of his helmet. Assessing me. Probably wondering why the hell I'm here and not their defenseman they traded for me.

I've known Graham Fisher as long as he's been alive. Being the son of one of my dad's closest friends, we were always together growing up.

Family barbeques.

Sporting games of any kind.

Holidays.

I don't know when things changed between the two of us, but we're going to have to get along just enough to make this whole team thing work.

"Fields." Graham skates up to me, stopping a good foot away from me.

"Fisher," I clip back at him.

He's the same height as me, but stockier. Graham has a scar that dissects his hard jaw—from an errant stick that caught him in college.

Why do I know these things about the man who hates me?

"Good to have you here," he tells me. "Think you're up to the task?"

"What's that supposed to mean?" I fire back at his jab. "Think I'm too old to be playing?"

Fisher rolls his eyes at me. "Are you always like this?"

"You're the one calling me old."

"I asked if you're up to the task. Not because you're old." Graham shakes his head at me. "We're not the best team in the league. It'd be stupid to pretend otherwise. You can't just skate out here like you own the place and expect everyone to fall at your feet because you've won a few cups."

Anger flashes through me. "Did I come in here acting like I own the place?"

"I know guys like you." Fisher skates a hair closer to me.

"Guys like me, huh?" I rest my gloved hands on my stick. "You don't know shit about me, Fisher."

"Oh, but I do."

A whistle blows, ending our standoff.

Fucking asshole. He doesn't know anything about me.

"Let's run some drills. See how we all work together," Coach Andrews bellows. "We've got a hard game tonight against San Jose, so let's focus on cleaning up our mistakes from the game against Arizona."

A few people groan and mutter under their breath.

The game against Arizona had more than a few mistakes. Puck control. Defense. Power plays.

Nothing went right for the Knights and they lost 7-2.

It was ugly.

Is this what I have to look forward to?

Practice is anything but fluid. Guys are missing easy passes, letting in goals that Nick would have stopped in his sleep, and making mistakes that any opposing team would take advantage of.

Fuck.

As the morning skate ends and I head back toward the visitors' locker room, at least one thing that feels familiar greets me that wasn't there earlier.

My jersey.

Fields is emblazoned in bright red on the back of the white jersey. A pair of crossed hockey sticks to look like swords for the Knights sits above the four that is stitched on the back.

At least I got to keep the same number. I don't know if I could ever give that up. My dad's old number from his playing days. I've never *not* played with this number. My own good luck charm of sorts.

While everything is changing, one thing hasn't. One thing is still familiar, even if I have a new team *and* new colors.

At least something doesn't suck today.

Chapter One

GRAHAM

"How you feeling, Flounder?" Jasper asks from his spot next to me on the bench. "All good?"

I jab my elbow into his side. "All good. We're not all old men in the league."

"Fuck you. I'm only thirty-four."

"Ancient in hockey years," Bode calls out from the other side of the locker room. "We'll be pushing you off the ice before we know it."

"Stop making fun of Jasper because he's old. You'll be lucky if you're playing in the league that long." Marcus rolls his eyes at us. Grabbing his stick and helmet, he leaves the locker room without giving us a backward glance.

"Someone woke up on the wrong side of the bed," Dax mutters.

"Or one of the girls is sick," I correct him.

"I can't imagine raising twin girls." Jasper shudders. "Do not sign me up for that."

"You'd first have to find someone that likes you enough to want to have kids," Bode prods at him.

"Do you think I could ask for a trade? I bet guys on

other teams don't have to deal with this shit," Jasper grumbles to himself.

"Aww. But then you'd miss us," I tell him.

Jasper rolls his eyes at me as he grabs his helmet and heads out to the ice for our first practice of the season.

"Hey guys."

I track the voice of the new guy as he walks into the locker room.

Noah Fields. One of the Knights' newest players. Even though the team traded for him last season, he didn't get that much playing time.

It's weird seeing him in our locker room. The red walls and floor with the Knights logo seemingly clash with him. The sleek, black lockers cut the brightness, but it still seems like Noah is seeking the attention of every man in the room.

I hate it.

Even still, he thinks he's God's gift to hockey.

The way he skates.

The way he wants everyone to treat him like a king.

The way he feeds off the attention of the crowd.

I hate it. I've hated it every minute since I started watching him play when he made it to the NHL. There's a cockiness there that I could never get past.

Noah Fields isn't the best player in the league. Not by a long shot, but with the way he carries himself, he thinks he is.

Asshole.

"You ready for a new season?" Dax asks him.

Noah shrugs, dropping his bag down into his locker on the other side of the room. Thank God for that at least.

"You know it. I'm ready for the season to start."

"Just remember, we're the red team," Bode tells him before he leaves the locker room on a laugh.

"Ouch. Not like I can forget."

Dax smacks him on the chest. "Ignore him. He probably didn't get laid last night."

"Is that common for him?" Noah asks, grabbing the back of his T-shirt and pulling it off and over his head.

Watching this exchange is mind-boggling to me. Noah wasn't here long enough last season to adjust. It's going to be weird having him here in my space now for the entire season.

My two worlds colliding.

It's not like I can control who the team trades for, but really? Noah Fields? They had to pick him up.

"You coming?" Dax calls out to me.

Looking around, I realize I'm one of the last guys in the locker room. I grab my helmet and stick and follow them out to the ice.

Breathing in the cold air helps to push all thoughts of Noah from my head. He can be the cocky player if he wants. I don't care.

Because stepping onto the ice is what I was born to do.

Looking up to the rafters, I take a minute to soak this feeling up. It's still new since it's only my third season with the Knights.

There's not much in the way of accolades hanging from the ceiling. Other teams have championship banners and retired numbers gracing their stands.

Us? Banners from our sponsors are about the only thing there.

I want to change that. With Coach Andrews coming in midway through last season, he didn't get a chance to make a lot of changes.

But he's hungry. I can feel it in the way he coaches us. He doesn't want the Knights to be a circled win anymore —a guaranteed victory for any team we might face.

The energy on the ice feels different as he calls everyone to center ice.

"Morning, gentlemen. I don't know about you, but I'm fired up that today is day one for the Knights."

A few guys break out into cheers and claps.

"I don't have to tell you what the pundits are saying. We all know what everyone thinks about the Knights."

"Rounding out the bottom of the league," Mickey, our defensive coach starts, "the Knights will likely get the first pick in the draft next season. With a change in coaching last season, the Knights didn't do much to show they are a contender for the playoffs. This season? Expect to see much of the same."

"Fuckers!" Bode shouts next to me.

"That is the last time they will ever say that about the Knights. I don't care what happened in the past. We're looking forward. What worked last season is not going to cut it this year. We're going to train harder. Faster. Longer. We're not going to be the laughingstock of the league anymore."

The lights of the arena reflect off Coach's glasses, making it hard to see his eyes. But there has to be a fire there. Ready to light the gas under every one of our asses.

Every single person on the ice is eating up his words. This is the passion that was missing from our last coach. This job was a paycheck to him. He didn't care if we won or lost. He did the bare minimum and called it a day.

Not Coach Andrews. I don't know if I've ever played for a coach that has as much drive as him. I fucking love it.

"Mark my words. The Knights will be in contention for the Stanley Cup in the next four years."

"Hell yeah!" someone shouts.

"It won't be easy though. Excuses aren't going to cut it around here. I want your very best every day. Knights

Hockey is going to become synonymous with grit, hard work, and determination."

The excitement from all the players is palpable. When Coach Andrews came in last season, it was more cleaning up and trying to make it through the season. Today feels like a fresh start. A new season of possibility.

"We're going to start practice today working with your line coaches and then run some drills. Like the start of every new season, you'll be feeling it, so make sure you take care of yourself, alright?"

Coach blows the whistle and dismisses us.

"Seems like Coach Andrews will be good."

Noah skates over to me, an excited look on his face.

"I think he'll be great for the Knights," I tell him. *Good? Just good?*

I have no idea what the future holds for our team, but I want to one-up the guy now standing in front of me.

Noah knows what it's like to play for a winning team, having won a few cups with Colorado. He doesn't get to skate in here and act like everything is going to be the exact same.

"Just got to put in the work like Coach said."

"You think I don't know that?" I fire back.

Noah throws his hands up. "Easy, man. I didn't mean anything by it."

"I know that we have to put in the work. I've been working hard every day since the Knights drafted me."

"I didn't say you weren't." An uneasy look washes over his face. "All I'm saying is it's going to take a team effort to get us where Coach says he can take us."

"And we can do it."

I skate off, not wanting to exchange any more words with him. Seriously, who does this guy think he is? Is he trying to angle for the captain's position?

Marcus has had that locked up for the last few years. The only thing that matters to him, outside his daughters, is hockey.

Noah can't come in here and take the baton from him. Hell no. I won't let it happen.

The Knights are my team. I'll protect them with everything I have. I don't want Noah to come in here and think he owns the place.

No way.

I don't care how good of a player he is. I'll be the better player just to prove him wrong.

Just wait and see.

Chapter Two

NOAH

"You said the place would be ready this week."

"We need another week, Mr. Fields. I promise, you'll have keys in hand by the end of next week."

I scrub a hand down my face. It's the last thing I wanted to hear, but I don't have a whole lot of options. "Thanks for the update."

Ending the call, I chuck my phone into my bag and head back to my locker.

"Everything okay?" Marcus asks, dropping down to sit next to me. His dark hair is wet, fresh from the shower after practice.

"Just another delay on my condo."

I was hoping to be moved in before the season started, but it got pushed back because of a delay. Something small that wouldn't take long to fix, I was told. Had I known it would take this long, I would've found something else. But getting traded so close to the Knights' season ending last year, I figured I'd be fine.

I was planning on going home to Denver anyway.

Now, I'm still in a less-than-stellar hotel trying to make things work.

"Shit, really?"

I nod, grabbing my water bottle and taking a swig. "Yup."

"You're more than welcome to come and stay in my spare room."

I quirk a brow at him. "I'm surprised you could say that with a straight face."

Marcus winces. "Just trying to do my captainly duties."

"I appreciate it." I clap him on the shoulder. "But the last thing you need is a teammate crashing with you and your kids. I'll be okay."

"You'll tell me if you're not?"

I nod. "Promise."

"Good. Now, what do you say to a drink? My mom has the girls, so I don't have to be home for another hour or two."

"Sounds good to me."

"HOW ARE YOU ADJUSTING TO NASHVILLE?"

It's hard to hear Marcus over the live music blasting throughout The Sin Bin. Even though we're off the more popular Broadway, aspiring musicians will play any set they can find. The low drone of voices does little to cover up the woman singing about what I'm guessing is an ex.

A hockey bar is no exception.

The lights are low in here with old, tin beer signs slapped up haphazardly on the walls. Photos of past Knights teams hang next to them. Neon lights glow as people all dressed up pass by, ignoring this small haunt.

Just the way I like it.

At my age, I couldn't care less about what's popular. I'd rather be able to sit down and have a drink without being hit on.

Because it's only a matter of time before someone spots me or Marcus in this grungy Nashville bar.

"It's been an adjustment," I tell him honestly. "I thought I'd have more time before the season ended, but then I was back home in Denver and—"

"And now you're here in a hotel that isn't quite cutting it?"

"Got it in one." I sip on my beer, only having one tonight. "I guess I assumed it'd be easier."

"Nah. I've never been traded, but it can't be easy. New team. New town. New home. I couldn't do it. I think I'd retire if they tried to trade me."

"Shit, really?" I ask. I try to hide the shock from my voice, but I can't.

Marcus Evans is one of the greatest players to ever suit up for Nashville. Even though they've been a team at the bottom of the league for years now, it wasn't because of Marcus.

"Too much upheaval. I've had enough of it to last a lifetime." Marcus fidgets with his empty ring finger before leaning back in our booth that's tucked away in the side of the bar. "I'd retire. Get some goats, maybe."

"Goats?" I snort over the gulp I just took, nearly choking on it. "Can't say that I picture you as a farmer."

"What?" Marcus throws his arms wide. "You don't think I could raise a pack of goats?"

"Are they called a pack of goats?" I ask him.

"Shit. I don't know. I'm sure Sadie does."

That gets a laugh out of me. "Is it bad your eight-year-old knows more than you?"

"Sadie is a genius. Just like her mom. She'll be running circles around me before long."

In the few months I was here last season, I learned as much as I could about my teammates. Marcus having two daughters is about as much as I know about him. The rest of his life is strictly off-limits.

"Maybe I should have retired. Stayed in Denver. No goats, but maybe a bunny."

"A bunny?" Marcus asks, sipping on his drink. "That's random."

I laugh. "Nick and I had a bunny. Well, Nick did, but we lived together and so it was mine too. Oreo."

"Fuck. Don't ever say you have a bunny around the girls, or I will see to it that you never play hockey again. They'll be asking for one as soon as they hear about it."

"Bunnies are easy," I point out.

Marcus shakes his head. "Don't care. Don't need something else to take care of."

"And you were offering me your spare room?"

"You're a grown man. I don't have to take care of you."

I sigh. "Maybe if I found a place earlier, it would have made the move easier."

"You think?" Marcus asks.

"I don't know. Might have helped to have someone help me find a place to live. My mom offered, but I don't know. I wanted to find a place that was mine."

When I was drafted by Colorado, my parents helped me find a place to live so I could focus on hockey. Getting traded to Nashville feels like the first time I've been away from everything I've ever known in life.

Even though I've lived away from my parents for the better part of my twenties, it felt like I was on my own for the first time. And I didn't want to have to rely on others to make it here.

"Well, I'm here if you need anything." Marcus glances at his watch. "Just don't call me after nine on weeknights to bail you out of jail."

"Who said anything about going to jail?"

That pulls a small smile from Marcus's usually hard face. "I'm only saying that my captainly duties have their limits."

"I'm not Bode." I laugh.

Now I get a real smile. "Bode would be the one to get arrested."

"Probably for public intoxication."

"If we do what Coach says we'll do,"—Marcus raps his knuckles on the wooden table between us—"Bode is definitely getting arrested."

I burst out laughing, drawing the eyes of a few people around us. "Thank God I'm not the captain and have to keep him in check."

"I'll just assign him to you to keep an eye on then."

"Okay, Marcus." I hold my beer bottle out to him in a toast. "If we win it all in a few years, I will gladly keep Bode's ass out of jail."

"I'll drink to that." He downs the remainder of his drink before pulling out his wallet. "Now, I have to go pick up some tutus for school tomorrow."

"Tutus?"

He nods. "Dance recital. I'll see you at practice."

I wave after him before finishing my own drink and heading out as well. Not wanting to go back to my dreary hotel room by myself, I stuff my hands in my pockets and walk around my new city.

This is one of those times it would be nice to have

someone to go home to. Hell, not even a someone, but an anyone. At least in Denver, I had Nick.

Even the guy I was kind of with has someone new. That was strictly a friends-with-benefits situation, but after my injury, I saw him less and less until he started dating someone else.

If I was really desperate, I'd download a hookup app to find someone. But I'm not. I wander around Nashville, taking in all the people going in and out of the bars. Neon lights are bright even in the early evening.

The hotel where I'm staying is a few blocks from the arena. This close, posters of the team hang on the street poles.

It's weird seeing my face up there in a red jersey. Just one of the many things I have to get used to.

That and playing with Graham Fisher. I don't know when things soured between us, but it seems like he has it out for me.

All I want to do is play hockey. That's it. I know I'm in the second half of my career. So sue me if I want to play hard and hopefully win another cup or two.

I only hope he can get on board. Because if not, it's going to be a long season. One that I won't be looking forward to.

Chapter Three

NOAH

I think that water spot is new. The one over by the wall? That's been there. But this one? It has to be new.

Christ. This is bad. My new place still isn't ready, and the only long-term hotel I could find near the rink is not the best of the best.

The worst of the worst is more like it. But with my condo being ready "any day now"—their words, not mine—no one wants to take on someone with an unknown end date.

Throwing the thin, flimsy excuse for a comforter off my legs, I head to the small bathroom to take a quick shower before practice.

The banging from the pipes tells me the water isn't going to get hot anytime soon, so it's going to be a fast one.

Jesus. This is not how I thought the start of this season would be going. I was hoping to be more settled here at this point. The bright side is that most of the team has welcomed me here.

Well, mostly everyone.

I still can't get a read on what crawled up Graham's

ass. Everyone, Marcus especially, has been more than welcoming to me.

All except Graham.

Shutting off the water, I run the sorry excuse for a towel over me before brushing my teeth and finding a clean set of clothes to put on.

The one plus side of living here is that I'm only a five-minute walk to the arena. No sense in driving when I don't have to.

Getting to see the arena like this, smack-dab in the middle of downtown Nashville, always lights me up. Fans always stop outside to take pictures on their way to the bars and I love it. Even though Nashville isn't the best of teams —yet—their fans still show up.

I guess things could be worse. At least I'm here and playing hockey. I could be done playing entirely. That's not something I'm ready to think about.

Flashing a wave to the security guard, I head toward the locker room. The vibe in this building is different from the Black Diamonds.

Back home, pictures of all the cups the team has won line the walls. Here? They're painted a bright red—maybe to distract you from the fact that there aren't any cup wins? —with our numbers in white over them.

I guess I should stop comparing this team to my old team. It's certainly not going to win me any friends.

Changing into my gear, I head out onto the ice for a few quick warm-up laps before practice starts. A couple of the guys are already out here as I get my feet under me.

The first few days of practice are the hardest. Getting back into shape for the season, no matter how much I trained during the offseason, is always difficult. But it's like learning to ride a bike.

And now, as Coach is calling everyone together for a scrimmage, it's second nature to me.

"Easy game, gentlemen. I want to see how well you all work together so we can work on our lines for the season."

Coach Mickey drops the puck as I take off, blowing past Graham who lined up opposite me.

Hell yeah.

I don't know why he hates me so much, but it amps up the need to beat him that much more.

Accepting the pass from Marcus, I deke Graham out and put the puck in the back of the net.

"Great pass!" I clap Marcus on the helmet as the defensive guys all huddle together to see what they did wrong.

"Even better goal."

Marcus was one of the first guys I gelled with since coming here, and it's apparent. The two of us work on the ice like we've been playing together for years, anticipating where the other will be and always there to set up an assist.

It makes me excited for the season to start.

Once play starts again, it's not as easy. The D line might have been caught with their pants down to start, but they're cleaning up their mistakes.

Graham is pushing me as I grab the puck and send it across the ice.

"Think you can beat me?" I egg him on.

"You know I can."

Bode shoots the puck back over to me and Graham is there to intercept it.

Fuck. I hate letting him get one over on me.

As we push back down the ice, our goalie blocks Graham's shot and deflects the puck to Marcus.

Even though this is supposed to be a friendly game, I

can't help but want to beat Graham. To wipe that cocky expression off his face anytime he looks at me.

Marcus and I are moving down the ice in perfect synchronicity as Bode moves along the boards. I shoot the puck to Marcus, and he flips it to Bode who lets it fly past the goalie for another score.

"Can I call dibs on playing with you two?" Marcus laughs as he claps Bode and me on the helmet.

"We'd be a tough line to beat," I tell them as I skate back over to center ice to take my position.

"Don't get so cocky. We'll stop you," Graham points out.

"Maybe if you did a better job defending the puck, we might not have scored on you. Two-nothing now, right? I think that's what the scoreboard says."

It's not what I should be saying, but damn, did it feel good. Until Graham's fist connects with my jaw.

"What the fuck, man?"

"Oh shit."

Those are the last words I hear before I return the punch to him. Noise fills my ears as the two of us throw fists, trying to connect with anything we can find purchase on.

"You're an asshole," I grit out as I try to push Graham to the ice.

"Maybe if you weren't such a dick about playing."

Graham's fist glances off my jaw and catches someone else before I'm being hauled off him.

A bruise is blooming on his cheek, and there's a small cut slicing his eyebrow. His dark brown eyes are filled with nothing but hate right now.

No doubt the same as mine.

I'm seething. If fire were coming out of my ears, I wouldn't be surprised.

Who does this guy think he is? It's his, what, third season? It's not like he plays for the best team in the league.

Hell, it's not like *I* play for the best team in the league anymore either, something I still haven't had time to get used to.

It fucking sucks.

"What the hell is wrong with you two? You're teammates. You shouldn't be going after one another."

"He started—"

"No," Marcus interrupts. "I don't want to hear it. I don't care what shit is going on between the two of you, but you need to work it out."

If possible, Graham looks even more pissed than I feel. It makes me want to punch him in the face.

Again.

But I can't. Not if I want to keep my position on this team.

Coach Andrews skates out to where the group of us are. His face is unreadable. Fuck. That is not a good thing.

"Coach. Sorry. Didn't mean to steal your thunder, but I couldn't take these guys being idiots anymore," Marcus tells him.

Andrews throws up his hands. "You took care of it about the same as I would. I appreciate your leadership skills."

Marcus nods. "Trying to do what I can, Coach."

"Appreciate it." Coach blows his whistle. "Suicides. Everyone. I'll let you know when you're done."

A collective groan echoes around the empty arena.

Fuck me.

I'm really making a great impression on my new team if this is what I bring down upon them. The worst drill in hockey—skating from one end of the rink to the blue line and back before going to center ice, then back, followed by the opposite blue line, then back again before doing it over the length of the entire ice.

I make sure to line up as far away from Graham as possible. Based on the pain in my jaw, I know there is going to be a wicked bruise there later.

Ignoring that pain, I listen for the whistle and put all of my anger and frustration into our drills.

By the time we're done, I have no idea how much time has passed, but I'm hurting. My thighs are burning and guys are grumbling as they head off the ice.

For more training in the weight room.

Fuck. This really is not how I wanted to start the season.

"Fields. Fisher. My office, please."

Coach Andrews doesn't say another word as he heads back down the tunnel. My eyes find Graham's across the ice and for once, he at least looks chagrined.

If it weren't for him, we wouldn't be in this situation in the first place.

He skates off first and I follow.

By the time I'm in the door after Graham, Coach Andrews is already seated behind his desk.

I haven't spent a lot of time in here, but it has more pictures of his family than it did last year. A TV takes up one wall with a dry erase board—my guess to plan out plays—and the other has a shelf filled with books, binders, and more pictures of him and his loved ones.

"What in the hell is going on between you two?" Coach asks. This time, there's a little less patience in his voice. "In all my years of coaching, I don't think I've ever seen two teammates go after one another."

"But—"

"No." Coach holds up a hand, interrupting whatever argument I was about to fire off at him. "The last thing we need is a division within the team. I don't want your dislike of one another to come between the team."

"It's my fault, Coach. I let my emotions get the better of me today and I'm sorry. It won't happen again."

My jaw drops. I mean, yes, it was Graham's fault because he threw the first punch, but I didn't expect him to so willingly accept the blame.

"Good. You're both exceptional players, and I would hate to see you two riding the bench because you can't control your emotions toward one another."

The threat hangs heavy in the air.

Get your shit together or you won't be playing.

"Yes, Coach," both of us answer at the same time.

"And to see to it that you start liking one another, I'll be working with the travel coordinator to make sure you two room together while we travel."

"Wait. What?" I ask.

"Rooming together. Standard operating procedure when traveling as a team."

"Yeah, but—"

Coach holds up his hand, effectively ending my argument. "No buts. I don't expect you two to be best friends by the end of the season, but you'll work together to help bring the Knights up to a level that we're all proud of. Understood?"

"Understood."

"Good. Now go before I make you do more suicides."

Chapter Four

NOAH

W here is that fucking Dopp kit?

My room is an absolute mess. Clean laundry is mixed in with the dirty laundry in a pile on my bed, and now I'm trying to get everything together in my away bag so I don't forget anything.

Fucking hell.

I really should try and get out of the contract I signed on my new place and try to find something that's ready now. If only I wouldn't be out the down payment.

The chirping from my phone on the bed distracts me.

A video call from my mom.

I don't think twice before sliding my thumb across the screen and answering. Her and Dad's faces fill the screen.

"Noah. Hi sweetheart," Mom says, a smile always present on her face. "Are you excited for the game tonight?"

She hasn't aged a bit. Her blonde hair is now styled in a short pixie cut, and glasses hide her blue eyes from the screen. Dad, however, has gone completely gray.

"I am. Ready to finally play together as a team, even if it's only preseason."

"Everything I'm hearing is that Coach Andrews is really going to turn the team around this year," Dad tells me. "You're lucky you get to play with him."

"It's not like I didn't have a great coach in Denver, Dad," I argue.

"Not saying you didn't. But I'd hate for you to squander such a great opportunity. Not a lot of guys get traded and then can say they'll help build a team from the ground up."

The enthusiasm in my dad's voice is obvious. I'm trying to get to that same level, but it's still hard. Especially thinking of who I'll be rooming with tonight.

Why does the thought of dealing with Graham Fisher turn me into a high schooler with an ax to grind?

"Is Graham looking out for you?" Mom asks. "I talked to Frankie the other day, and she hadn't really heard anything from him."

I groan, scrubbing a hand down my face. No use in hiding what they'll eventually hear. My parents and their friends, Dad's old teammates, are the biggest gossips in the world. I already talked to Nick about it, which means Angie heard, and within a few days, my parents will be hearing it through the grapevine.

Might as well rip the bandage off now.

"Not really. We kind of got into it at practice the other day."

That has both of their faces drawing up tight in confusion. "A fight?" Dad asks. "You two?"

"Noah Jackson Fields. You shouldn't be fighting with your teammates," Mom chides.

I wince at her admonishment. Doesn't matter how old

you are, there's nothing like getting told off by your mother.

"I didn't mean for it to happen. It just did."

"When did things go so wrong between the two of you?" Mom asks. "I always thought you were friends growing up."

"As much as we could be when he was so much younger than me."

"Look," Dad interjects. "I know part of this might have to do with the fact that you're having a hard time adjusting still since being traded."

I try not to roll my eyes at him. Not when he's only trying to be helpful and give advice.

"But look at this as an opportunity."

"An opportunity?" I ask.

"Yes," Mom agrees. "Just because you aren't a captain anymore doesn't mean you can't act like one. Getting into fights with a teammate? That's not like you. Step up and show the Knights the caliber of player you really are. Remind them why they traded for *you*."

"Okay, Mom."

"Don't use that exasperated tone with me, son."

"Mom! I wasn't."

I totally was, but I was trying to hide it. I should know by now that I can't get anything past my mom. Changing the phone to my other hand, I spot my Dopp kit on the other bed and grab it.

"Noah. Are you still in that hotel room?" Dad asks, eyeing the room behind me the best he can on a tiny screen over a thousand miles away.

"My condo isn't ready yet."

"Is that really the best you can find?" Mom asks. "Honestly. Getting into fights? Staying in a run-down hotel? Noah. Are you having a midlife crisis or something?"

"Tenley."

"Mom."

"What?" She moves away from the screen. "I can't worry about my son?"

"He's fine, Tenley."

"Look, I have to go. We're going to be heading out soon and I don't want to be late. I love you guys."

"We love you, son. Make sure you get into your place soon, okay? I can only hold Mom off for so long," Dad tells me, a smirk on his face.

"I heard that." Mom pops up behind him. "Play well, sweetheart. Love you."

"Love you. Bye."

I end the call before I can get my ass handed to me again.

Chucking everything I need into my overnight bag, I sling it over my shoulder and walk out the door. Their advice wasn't bad.

I'm better than this. Better than stewing over what I lost and fighting it—and teammates—because it's not what I know. What I'm used to.

Hell, if that happened during a game, we'd be the laughingstock of the league for years to come.

I need to get my head on straight. The Knights is my team.

Graham Fisher is my teammate. I can make this work.

I have to.

Because otherwise, I have no other option. When I got traded, Nashville put a no-trade clause in my contract. After this, if they don't want me, that's it. I'm cut.

No other team would want me.

Fake it 'til I like Graham Fisher is going to be my new motto.

I can make it work.

Right?

"THAT WAS A GREAT GOAL TONIGHT," Graham tells me. It's hard to miss the awkward intonation in his voice.

"Thanks." I drop the bag onto the hotel room bed as I watch him shrug out of his suit jacket. There's a stilted silence between the two of us. "D looked good."

Graham nods back to me. "Thanks."

God, is it always going to be this hard?

Be the bigger person, Noah.

Graham extended an olive branch, so there's no use in throwing it back in his face. I need to ignore the voice in the back of my head saying that he started it all.

Bigger person.

"We played well as a team, even if we lost. Defense is looking good."

"Yeah, thanks. We'll have to clean some stuff up in practice."

Awkward silence.

Fuck. This might be harder than I thought it would be.

Even though it was a short trip to St. Louis tonight, we're flying out on a quick road trip out west before coming home.

Meaning it's our first night together as roommates. The first of many. We need something to break the ice.

Glancing around the hotel room—one that doesn't have water spots and has bedspreads that actually might keep you warm—I spot the minibar.

"Do you want something to drink?"

Graham blows out a breath. "Oh, fuck yes."

Snorting a laugh, I head to the minibar and grab a

handful of tiny bottles. Even if it won't get us drunk, it'll at least help take the edge off.

"I'll take the bourbon if there's one," Graham tells me.

Dropping half a dozen or so bottles on the bed, I grab two of the same and hand one to him. "At least you have good taste in booze."

"Cheers to that."

We clink bottles, unscrew the caps, and knock them back.

"Damn. That feels good."

Graham wipes his lips before holding out his hand for another.

"Easy." I hand him one of the golden bottles of rum. "This is all we've got."

"You know," Graham starts, "we could always go to the bar and get an actual drink."

I flop back onto the bed, kicking my shoes off. "Nah. I'm good hanging out up here."

Graham takes a spot on his bed, mirroring my position. "I am too. There's something about not having to be on with all the guys."

"Really? I thought you'd be all about that."

Graham shifts, sitting at the edge of the bed, propped back on his elbows. "Why's that?"

"Because it's the start of your third season. You don't want to be out sowing your wild oats?"

Bursting out in laughter, Graham sips on his drink. "What are you, eighty? You sound like Gigi."

"I swear, your grandma can get away with anything." I laugh.

"Actually, I don't think Gigi would say that. She'd just say why aren't you out picking people up at the clubs? She'd be disappointed the two of us are up here and not going out."

"I'm well past that point in my career. Why don't you want to go out with the guys?"

Graham grabs another bottle and takes a small sip. "I don't know. It's never been my thing. I always wanted to focus on hockey."

"Guess that's one thing we have in common."

"My dad always said it's the most important thing. Don't get caught up in the lifestyle and forget why you're there."

I laugh, sipping on a bottle of vodka. It's cheap, burning as it goes down. But it helps to loosen my tongue. "Maybe we should remind Bode of that."

"By the time he's done with his career, he'll have slept with every woman in Nashville."

I point at Graham. "And that is why I don't feel the need to go out with the guys."

"Although it is fun to watch him get shut down every now and again."

"Well, you wouldn't see me getting shut down."

Graham rolls his eyes. "Why, because no one can say no to you?"

I shake my head and ignore his reaction. Apparently all we need is alcohol for things to soften between us. "Because I doubt any of the guys would go to the gay bars with me."

"Marcus and Jasper would. Dax tends to be the only person to keep Bode in line, so he'd likely go with him."

"Good to know."

See? I can be the bigger person and learn things from Graham that I might not have gleaned otherwise about my teammates.

The silence comes back, but this time, it's not nearly as heavy as before. It has some of the tension loosening in my chest.

Maybe this won't be so bad. Playing hockey is hard. Having to make nice with your enemy to keep playing?

I can do this.

"Want to watch the Vancouver game?" Graham asks.

"Sure."

He flips the TV on and finds the game.

"Figure we can learn about our opponent and get a leg up on them."

"Could even help the guys out in practice. Get back in their good graces."

Graham grabs another tiny bottle and swallows the amber liquid down in one go. "I'll drink to that."

By the time the game is over, even though we haven't talked much, the tension has eased. Who knew all you needed was a few tiny bottles of hotel liquor and a hockey game to break the ice?

Chapter Five

NOAH

"**A**re you serious?"

"I apologize, but the building didn't pass inspection due to bad electric work, and it'll be a few more months before it gets corrected."

"And there's nothing you can do until then?" I scrub a hand across my forehead. "You said it would only be until the end of the week."

"I'm sorry, Mr. Fields, but the building cannot be occupied until final inspection."

"If that day ever comes."

I end the call and toss my phone into my bag, not caring that I was more curt than I should have been. This is not what I needed today. I thought for sure that I'd be able to get moved in once we were back from our road trip, yet I'm still waiting through another seemingly endless delay.

I figured a brand-new high-rise in the city would be the perfect place for me. Quiet because it wouldn't be filled to capacity. A doorman to prevent any wayward fans from finding me. And most important, a place to rest my head that is my own. It's why I kept waiting on this place. Well after last season even.

Now, I have no place to go except the cheap hotel that I chose only because it's close to the rink.

Can one thing go right since being traded?

I head toward the weight room for the optional morning workout before our preseason game tonight, hoping to clear my head. Half the guys are here, but I know more will come later.

The treadmills are empty—the perfect way to pound out this annoyance. Keeping up with regular physical therapy during the offseason has helped me make leaps and bounds in my recovery.

My knee feels like it's brand-new. Knowing it can handle the strenuous pace I set, I start the treadmill and take off on the grueling workout.

Guys start coming in, shooting the shit with each other. A few give me a wave, while others head toward their preferred workout station.

I hate that I still don't feel like a part of the team. Sure, I have the few guys that I hang out with every now and then, but it feels different.

A bridge I'm not quite sure how to cross.

Graham enters the weight room, heading straight toward me. At least that's something that's changed. It doesn't feel outright hostile with him now.

More like simmering annoyance.

He gives me a nod as he gets onto the treadmill next to me. Eyeing my own speed, he sets his one notch above mine and takes off.

Maybe I was wrong on that whole hostile feeling. I kick my own speed up one above his.

Two can play at that game.

Glancing over at him, I see a smirk playing on the

corner of his mouth. Something I shouldn't be noticing. Because…why am I finding it sexy?

I push those thoughts from my head as Graham jabs his finger at the screen. He punches his treadmill up as high as it can go. I follow.

The burn in my legs feels good as I push myself harder than I have in months. The hard beat of my feet reverberates through my entire body, pushing me even harder. Fuck, does it ever feel good.

Like I can do what I was supposed to.

Play hockey and not just sit on the bench.

Maybe having Graham around is a good thing. I shudder at the thought. Because that is not something I would have thought at any point.

"Think you can keep it up, old man?" Graham taunts me from his spot.

"See if you can." I send a wink his way, and I don't miss the way he stumbles over his feet for the briefest of seconds.

I pump my arms, pushing myself even harder to keep up with him. I've got almost seven years on him. I might not be the fastest guy anymore after years of playing, but if I can push him to keep up, why wouldn't I?

Until a voice startles me out of my thoughts.

"Jesus. Can you two stop making everything into a competition? I don't need you idiots hurting yourselves before the season even starts." Marcus groans. "You're worse than the girls."

Changing the pace to a brisk walk, I slow down as Graham does the same thing beside me.

"Gotta make sure our top center is in shape," Graham chirps.

"More like dead on the ice tonight if you two keep this up," Marcus fires back.

"I know exactly how hard to push myself."

Marcus gives me a weary look. "This feels more like a pissing match to me."

"Nah." I wave him off. "Just trying to work out some stress. That's all."

"Did you hear about your condo?" Marcus asks, dropping onto the weight machine in front of us.

"Yeah. Not good news."

"What's not good news?" Graham asks, inserting himself into the conversation. Sweat drips down from his face. He lifts his shirt to wipe it off, and I do my best to ignore the brief flash of his abs I get.

I must really be in a weird place right now if I'm eyeing his abs. Maybe I need to find someone to release some of this pent-up energy instead of going for a workout.

Or just getting a different kind of workout.

"My condo is delayed again. Probably another couple of months."

"Shit, really?" Marcus asks, setting the weight bar on the rest and sitting up.

"You still don't have a place to live?" Graham asks, resting his hands on his hips.

"It's fine. No big deal."

"Don't listen to him." Marcus ignores me. "It is a big deal. I can't have you playing like crap."

"Hey!" I interject. "I'm not playing like crap."

Marcus studies me, then turns his focus to Graham. Before looking back at me, his face lights up.

"Why don't you stay with Flounder?" Marcus asks. "He has room and it's close to the rink."

"What? Why me?" Graham asks. His face goes hard, like me living with him would be the worst thing in the world.

Except…it might just be the worst thing in the world.

"It's fine." I take a swig from my water bottle and toss it back onto the bench. "I'm good where I am."

Marcus raises a brow at me like he's not buying my crap. Having young kids must decrease your bullshit meter. "You told me the other night how shitty the place you're staying is."

"Well, not shitty per se…"

"Look, Flounder has a spare room. You need a place to stay. Suck it up, Noah. I don't want you turning into a shitty player because you're not sleeping at night."

"Fuck you. I'm playing just fine."

"Then keep it that way," Marcus tells me.

"How do you know I still have a spare room?" Graham asks Marcus. "I could have done something with it."

"Have you? Because I was at your place only a few weeks ago and it was sitting empty."

Graham mutters under his breath at Marcus's words.

"I can keep looking. Ignore Marcus."

Graham shakes his head at me, scoffing. "Have you met him? He's scary. I don't want him coming for my ass for ignoring him. Come by after practice."

"Really?"

"Yes. I have a spare room with a bed. Don't make me tell you twice."

"Fine. Thanks."

"Don't mention it."

Maybe I could figure something else out, but with us leaving late tomorrow night for a road game the following day, I don't really have many options. Hell, I could get my mom to come out and find something for me, but she has work. Piper, too.

They're about the only two people I would trust to find me a good place to live. Which, at this point, the bar is low.

Leaving me with my only option.

Graham fucking Fisher.

GRAHAM

THIS IS QUITE POSSIBLY the worst idea ever. Not that it was my idea to begin with. But when the captain suggests something, it's not really a suggestion. I don't want to get on Marcus's bad side, so here I am. Clearing out my second bedroom to make room for Noah Fields.

Maybe Noah'moving in with me will help mend the fences between the two of us. I have no idea where things went wrong. It doesn't help that I hit him just right and took him out of the game. It wasn't intentional, just a bad luck of the draw for him.

Things defrosted after our first road trip. Not entirely thawed, but enough for our coaches and team to see that we won't repeat what happened at practice.

But having to room with him both on the road and at home? I haven't lived with anyone since my freshman year of college. I like having my own space. After a hard practice or a tough loss, the silence of my own space was always just what I needed. To not be around people and decompress by myself.

The buzzer from the living room has me tossing the last pillow on the bed and heading out to let him up.

Nerves start to swarm as I wait for my new roommate to come up. The building isn't new, but my place was recently renovated. It's what made it so appealing when I got drafted by the Knights out of college.

A soft knock echoes around the living room. I open the door, and there's Noah, with one bag slung over his shoulder and a duffle at his feet.

"Hey." I sweep the front door open and watch as he brushes past me.

"Graham." Noah nods at me as he drops his bags on the floor in the entryway and heads inside.

A flat screen TV takes up one wall in the living room with every gaming system you could ever dream of. One couch faces the TV with a lone chair nearby with its back toward the windows. Given the small size of the condo, I don't have a dining room table and opted for barstools in the kitchen. It's not like I entertain a lot of the guys on the team.

"It's not much, but you've got your own room and bathroom."

Noah smiles at me. "I know you don't really want me here, so thanks. It's better than a hotel room, that's for sure."

"Hey, make yourself at home. Definitely better than a hotel. Want to unpack or want to play some video games?"

It's an olive branch if I've ever extended one. This place is my haven from the world. From the press and all the negatives I've heard over the last few seasons about the Knights.

No point in my making things harder for both of us by ignoring Noah.

My teammate.

And my new roommate.

That's going to take some getting used to.

"How about some video games?" Noah walks into the living room. "You got anything to drink?"

"Uhh." Heading into the kitchen, I open the fridge to a few pre-cooked meals, moldy veggies, and a six-pack of beer. Thank God. Maybe a little buzz might help break the proverbial ice.

"Beer okay?"

"Sure."

I hand one to Noah and he drops down onto the couch. Following suit, I grab the controllers, hand him one, and choose a hockey game that we'll both be able to play. Firing up the game, we pick our players and start playing.

The silence doesn't feel as heavy. Like we're not going to go after one another for some stupid reason.

A memory from when we were kids slams into me. One I haven't thought of in years.

It was one of the first times I was ever on the ice. Noah was the first one of us to play hockey, and I wanted to play. Just like Noah.

I didn't start out with a lot of skill, but Noah had patience. I couldn't have been more than seven at the time, and he was already in high school, starting for the varsity team. He could have brushed me off, but he didn't. Noah showed me all his tricks on how to train to be a better player.

I don't think I'd be here if it weren't for him. To be here with him now after all of these years? It's weird.

A thought that must be all over my face based on Noah's next words.

"This is weird, right?" Noah asks. His character passes the puck to me, and I fire it into the goal. "Nice goal."

"Thanks. If only it were this easy in real life, right?" I laugh, setting down the controller to grab a sip of my beer. "Kind of weird, yeah."

"This is only temporary, I promise."

I wave him off. "It's fine. Like Marcus said, I have the room."

"Do you?" Noah turns around. "Because no offense, but this is one tiny-ass condo."

"Hey, I'm still on a rookie contract. If I'm going to get traded, I don't want to worry about selling a huge place."

"Yeah…" Noah turns his focus back to the game. "It fucking blows."

I wince. "Sorry. I wasn't thinking."

"It happens to all of us." Noah shrugs. "At least I don't come with extra baggage."

"What kind of baggage would that be?" I ask.

"A bunny."

I nearly spit out my beer. "A bunny."

Noah looks at me like I have three heads. "You have to know that Nick and I used to have a bunny."

"You did? I so did not know about this."

Noah smiles and picks up his controller as we restart the game. "Oreo. He was mostly Nick's, but we lived together, and I liked the little guy."

"Do I need to get you a bunny now to keep the peace?"

"Nah." Noah does a complicated spin move and ends up getting another goal. "As long as you let me have my pre-game naps, I'll be okay."

"Duly noted." I nod. "Anything else I should know?"

"Do you really want to know?" Noah eyes me before turning his attention back to the TV.

"Yes."

He pauses the game. "Well, I enjoy cooking, and based on your reaction when you opened your fridge, you didn't have much in there. If you help with groceries, I can cook for us."

"Okay."

"Other than that, hockey is twenty-four seven."

"Same," I agree.

Noah laughs. "That makes us sound pretty pathetic, right?"

"We probably need more of a life."

"Eh. If it gets us a championship, I can have a life after hockey. Enjoy it more then."

I wince. Hearing this and how I reacted at practice the other day? Considering hockey is my sole focus, it wasn't the best way to handle things. "Look, I'm sorry about practice. I don't really know what came over me and I snapped."

"It's okay."

I shake my head. "It's not. I don't really think I made it easy on you to adjust to a new team and I'm sorry."

"Consider us even. You're helping me out with a place to stay until my condo is ready. If it ever is."

"Deal." I pick at the label on my beer bottle. "Are you going to the team picnic this weekend?"

"Planning on it."

"Maybe we could ride over together?" I hate how unsure I sound. It's not like it's a hardship. We live together. It'd be stupid *not* to go together.

This whole thing of being nice to Noah is new. Something I'll have to get used to.

"Sounds good." Noah stands, heading to the kitchen and dropping his empty bottle in the blue recycling bin. "I don't know if you like live music or not, but we could always go downtown after?"

I nod. "Yeah, I'm always up for that. One of the good parts about Nashville."

Noah scrubs a hand over the back of his head. "Cool. I'm pretty beat, so I think I'm going to go get settled and hit the sack."

"Alright."

He shoves a hand through his hair. "Listen, I appreciate this."

"Don't mention it."

Noah shakes his head, shoving his hands into his sweats and leaning against the counter. "Hopefully it won't be too long. No more than two months."

Standing, I head toward him and lean across the bar. "Take as long as you need. It's not like I had anyone using the room."

"Thanks."

A couple of months. We can handle not killing each other for a couple of months. Hell, maybe we'll even become friends by the time he leaves.

Let's hope for that.

Chapter Six

GRAHAM

MARCUS

Team picnic at 3 sharp. I expect to see you
all there

BODE

Coach said it wasn't required

MARCUS

It is for us. You're the alternate captain. I
expect you—all of you—to be there

JASPER

Keep it in your pants for a night, Bode

BODE

I'm offended you think I can't

GRAHAM

It's only because we know you

DAX

I'm surprised the thing hasn't fallen off

NOAH

I don't feel like I know you well enough yet
to have a comment on this

BODE

I'm not a playboy like they're leading you to
believe

MARCUS

Thanks for the laugh, Bode. I needed it

BODE

Asshole

DAX

Just show up on time and maybe don't
bring your date

BODE

When was the last time I ever brought a
date to one of these things?

NOAH

Shit. Are we supposed to bring someone?

MARCUS

Just bring your new roomie. Assuming you
two haven't killed one another by then

Hey!

NOAH

Fuck you, man

We're getting along great

MARCUS

I'll need to see it to believe it

NOAH

We played video games the other night

JASPER

True male bonding

BODE

Remind me never to get a roommate.

MARCUS

You could use one to rein you in

BODE

See if I show up tonight

DAX

If you don't show up and Coach makes us
run suicides, I'll be pissed

BODE

Ugh, fine. You big baby. And you could use
some more training if you can't do suicides

DAX

Fuck off

MARCUS

And I'm out. I can't handle you guys when
you're like this

NOAH

Are they always like this?

Anyone?

"I'm assuming they're always like this if no one will answer me?" Noah asks, walking out of his room and into the living room. He's in a pair of loose-fitting jeans and a Knights pullover.

"I'd like to say no they're not, but they are." I laugh.

"Kind of makes me feel at home."

"Really?"

Reaching into the fridge, I grab a bottle of water and

take a quick glug. Looking at him, I hold mine up, asking if he wants one.

Noah nods. "Thanks. It's just like the guys at home. Makes me feel like I'm finally part of the team."

"We're lucky to have you."

"You don't have to be nice now that we're living together."

I bark out a laugh, grabbing my hat off the counter. "I'm not. Trust me."

"Really?" Noah quirks an eyebrow in my direction.

"Are you going to make me say it?"

"Well, now I have to hear this."

"Ugh. I hate you," I groan. "I guess you're not as bad as I thought you were."

A look of shock washes over Noah's face. "Wow. Here I thought I'd never change your mind about me."

"You were kind of a cocky asshole when you started."

"I was not!" Noah looks affronted. "Just because you don't have my raw, natural talent."

"I take it back. You're still just as bad."

Noah holds his hands up in defense. "Kidding."

"I remember wanting to play with you so bad when you came home from college, but whenever I texted, you were always busy. I felt like a pest you were trying to blow off. I guess I thought you were this ass who didn't want to be around his dad's friend's kid."

"Really? You know I would never have actually blown you off. I was just busy with my own schedule."

I laugh. "I know that *now*. It was hard as a middle schooler to realize it. Hockey takes up your entire life."

Noah nods in agreement. "It really does."

"And I guess I could never really separate you from that time."

Noah holds out his hand for me. "Then I guess I'm glad we're friends now."

I point a finger at him. "Don't make me regret it."

"I'll try not to. Now, are we going to this barbecue or what?"

BY THE TIME we make it to the farm where the party is being hosted, it's hopping. Everyone from the team is here. Guys I've been skating with since I started here and a few rookies who were drafted this year.

Executives from the front office came. Some I recognize, some I don't.

The sprawling field is bustling with activity. There's face painting, a bounce house, a petting zoo, plus an ice cream truck and a full bar and buffet with more food than I could ever imagine.

Guys are standing around chatting with loved ones as kids run around, laughing and screaming.

"Damn. The Knights go all out," Noah says from his spot next to me.

I shake my head. "This is the first year they've done anything like this."

"Really? I wonder why now."

I nod, pointing toward the bar to lead us to get a drink. "I think Coach Andrews is really trying to change the environment of the team."

Noah and I each grab a beer and hang out toward the side of the crowd. "How was it under the old coach? I don't know if I've ever asked."

"Different. He only cared about wins and losses, and even then, not that much. Didn't really encourage a team atmosphere. He was on his way out and really didn't give a shit."

"Wow." Noah cracks open his beer and takes a sip. "I don't know if I would have lasted playing under someone like that."

"It sucked. So if Coach Andrews wants to do something like this to increase team morale, I'm all for it."

"Even with me?" Noah elbows me in the side.

I turn and study him. I don't know why I ever thought he was the dickhead I painted him to be. Maybe I was just jealous of him and his talent and that I had to work harder to achieve everything I've gotten. This Noah—the one I'm getting to know—could be someone I'm friends with.

Real, actual friends with.

"You're not so bad." I laugh.

"Ringing endorsement, Flounder."

"Damn. I never thought I'd see the two of you being cordial."

I snort over my beer as Bode sidles up to the two of us.

"I never thought I'd see the day when you didn't have a date on your arm," I fire back at him.

"You wish you were me, Flounder." He gives me a smarmy grin. "I clean up with the ladies. You could take a page from my playbook."

"No, thanks," I tell him.

"You don't have anyone special?" Noah asks, casual as ever with a pair of dark sunglasses covering his eyes.

"Have you seen me bring anyone around?"

"No, but that doesn't mean you don't go to their place."

I shrug a shoulder. "No. My main focus is hockey. There will be plenty of time to settle down."

"God. Listen to you two." Bode winces. "I'll be six feet

under when I settle down. I can't even look at you right now."

He goes off to find other guys as Marcus and Jasper take his place.

"How goes the living situation?" Jasper asks, looking out across the farm. "You two getting along?"

"We're good," we answer at the same time.

"Damn. You two really are getting along," Marcus tells us. "If you two had us doing any extra drills, I would've forced you into a room until you kissed and made up."

"What a captain you are, Marcus." Noah is laughing, but Marcus's words have a weird feeling washing over me.

What that feeling is, I can't exactly pinpoint.

"You bring the girls?" Noah asks Marcus.

"They're around here somewhere with my mom. No doubt inciting mayhem."

"I don't know how you do it," Noah tells him. "I know I couldn't."

"It's because you're a kid most days yourself," I tell him.

"Dick!" But Noah doesn't mean it if the grin on his face is anything to go by.

"Not all it's cracked up to be," I hear Marcus mutter as the conversation continues around me. I still can't shake that weird feeling at his earlier words as he, Jasper, and Noah go meet up with some of the other guys.

Leaving me to my wayward thoughts.

Thoughts that I have no idea where they're coming from. Kissing and making up with Noah? Why is my brain latching on to the kissing part? With Noah?

A man.

Draining the last sips of my beer, I drop the empty can into a bin and grab another.

Get a grip, I tell myself.

Maybe it's the heat that's getting to me. *It's a nice day, you idiot.*

Maybe it's because I'm getting to know him better. That has to be it. That I like the guy. As a teammate. And my roommate.

That's it. Nothing else.

Taking a cool sip of a fresh beer helps to calm the buzzing flowing inside of me. The only thing I need to be worried about—focusing on—is hockey. That's it.

That's how it's always been.

I'm not like Bode who takes someone new to bed every chance he can get. That's not me and it's never been me.

Glancing around, I see my assistant defensive coach. Except what I see next stops me in my tracks. Someone else walks up to him and gives him a kiss.

Husband? Boyfriend? Partner?

I don't know who this person is to him, but now it's taking those earlier feelings and throwing gasoline on them. I shouldn't be staring, but I can't tear my eyes from them. From the tender way he holds him to the soft look in his eyes. They're pressed close together, not caring that anyone here could see them.

I don't know why I can't look away.

Fuck. Fuck.

When they break apart, Mickey looks my way.

"Graham."

"Hey, Coach." I throw an awkward hand in the air. "Sorry. Didn't mean to stare."

I walk over toward him and extend a hand to him.

"Darren, this is—"

The man with him, a shorter man with dark hair, gives me a big smile. "I know exactly who this is. I'm a big fan of your mom."

I return his smile. "I am too."

"It's not every day a woman wins a few Super Bowls as a head coach."

I sip my beer, thankful this man cut the tension that was going to swallow me whole. "She is pretty badass."

"No disrespect to your dad," Mickey tells me. He's a taller, more fit version of his husband—I now see the glinting band on his ring finger. "He was a great player, but we love seeing the underdog succeed."

"He'll be the first to tell you that she deserves all the praise over him any day."

It's how it's always been. My parents have one of the best relationships I've ever witnessed. Their love story is a thing of beauty, and it's why I always focused on hockey. Seeing how much they love each other always made me want that.

I never wanted to settle for anything less than what they had. It was always easier to focus on what I could control, like hockey. I couldn't do hockey *and* a relationship, so I took the easier option.

"I could stand here and gush over your mom all day. Breaking barriers and shattering glass ceilings, but I'm sure you've heard it all," Darren tells me. "It really was nice to meet you, though. I don't meet a lot of Mickey's players."

I hold out my hand for him to shake. "It's nice to meet you too. I'm glad Coach Andrews organized this."

Mickey nods. "I think he's going to bring some big changes to Nashville."

"I feel it too," I agree. "All I want is to be part of a winning organization."

It's not a lie. No player grows up dreaming about being a part of the league's worst team. Having had a front-row seat to the Mountain Lions' greatness growing up, I didn't want anything less.

So when I was drafted by the Knights, it wasn't the best

situation. But I couldn't complain. Not when I was living out my dream.

"We don't want to keep you," Darren interrupts my thoughts. "But it was wonderful to meet you."

"Yeah. You too."

I wave at them as they link hands and head off into the party.

Once again, leaving me with these swirling thoughts that I have no idea what to do with.

Chapter Seven

NOAH

"You guys up for going out?" Bode pops up between the seats as the bus pulls into the parking lot of the arena.

"Bode, it's almost ten," I tell him.

"So? You heard Coach—optional morning skate tomorrow because we won back-to-back. That deserves to be celebrated, Fields."

It's weird hearing him call me Fields. For so long with the Black Diamonds, I was always Strawberry. Did I hate it then? Yes. Now, I miss it. I miss the familiarity of the team and guys. They became a second family to me.

Something that still feels like it's missing here since I was thrown into the deep end with only a few weeks before our season ended last year.

"C'mon, man. You can't say no." Dax tugs a baseball hat over his head, getting ready to head off the bus. Being one of the newer, faster players we have, the fans in Nashville love him. Whenever we go out, he tends to draw a lot of attention.

Considering how shy he is? He isn't a fan of it.

"Aren't you guys tired?"

Having just gotten back from a stretch of preseason games on the road, the very last thing I want to do is go out and hang with the guys.

Maybe this is why I haven't bonded with any of them, I chide myself.

"I'm out." Marcus hefts his bag over his shoulder before fishing out his keys and jogging down the aisle of the bus once it comes to a stop. "I'll see you guys later."

"Okay, how come he doesn't have to come out?" I whine.

"Because he has a family to get home to," Bode points out.

"So, because I'm single I have to come?" I ask Jasper.

"Yes. Even I'm going out, so you can't say no."

"Ugh. Fine," I grumble.

"Flounder. You in?" Bode calls back to Graham.

He shrugs a shoulder as he bounds off the bus. "I wouldn't mind going out. If you're buying."

"Cheap ass."

"I'm happy to stay at home."

Bode groans. "Fine, I'll buy. I know a great club with a VIP section we can get into."

He's firing away a message on his phone as Graham sidles up to me. "Think we can cut out after two drinks?"

I laugh as we head to my truck. My phone buzzes in my pocket. I'm guessing it's the address Bode just sent to all of us.

"I'm planning on it."

"Good."

By the time we get to the club—some place on Broadway—Bode is there waiting for us as we're shown behind a velvet rope to a set of stairs. Following behind him, we enter a dark room with low, blue lights that are reflecting off the mirrored walls.

A bar takes up the back wall with a few servers slinging mixed drinks. Some of the guys are already up here with women on their arms.

Grabbing a seat on the velvet benches that line one of the walls, Jasper, Dax, Graham, and I all drop down onto the cushy seats.

"Who wants what?" I ask.

I listen to their drink orders before heading off to the bar and waiting behind a few of the guys. I don't miss the way the bartender's eyes latch on to mine.

"What can I get you?" he asks as I lean against the solid wood bar.

"Two IPAs and two old-fashioneds."

"You got it, babe."

I watch as he makes the drinks before Bode is pushing his way to the front. "Make sure you come back and see me now."

"Thanks."

"Someone looked interested," Jasper tells me as I set the drinks down on the low table in front of us.

I shake my head as I sip on my drink. "Nah. He was just trying to get better tips."

"I don't know." Jasper peers around me toward the bar. "He definitely is checking you out."

"Leave him alone," Graham whispers. It's so quiet, I'm the only one that hears him. When I cut a quick glance at him, his eyes are hard.

What in the world?

"Why aren't you trying to pick anyone up, Dax?" I ask, changing the subject.

"Not interested in anyone specific." His eyes roam over the VIP room. More of the guys have arrived, filling the small space.

"Does that mean there is someone you could be interested in?"

"No." He answers too fast. There's definitely a story there, but Jasper won't let me get it because he is still on the bartender. "Go get me another drink."

"Why me?" I scoff.

"Because the bartender thinks you're cute and I need another beer."

I glance over to his still half-full drink. He definitely knows what is going on with Dax, but I let it slide. Maybe once Dax likes me more, he'll open up to me.

That's something I want more than I thought possible. I want these guys to become my family out here. If I have to go get Jasper another beer to keep the heat off Dax, I'll do it.

"Already back for seconds?"

The guy is leaning over the bar, giving me a slow perusal. His blue eyes are playful, and his blond hair is styled into a perfect, slicked-back mohawk.

"Another IPA, please."

He smiles at me as he grabs another glass to pull the drink. "You don't seem like a beer guy."

"Getting it for a friend. I like bourbon."

"Something sweet and fiery, huh?" he asks, waggling his brows at me. "Kinda like me?"

"Subtle." I smile back at him.

"What can I say? I see what I want and go for it."

"And what do you want?"

"You."

Any other night and I'd be taking this guy up on his

offer. But tonight? Tonight, I'm not feeling it. Maybe it's because I want to stay and hang with the guys, or maybe I'm just over my messing-around phase.

"Not tonight. Sorry, man."

Dropping a twenty into the tip jar, I grab Jasper's drink and head back to the table. The second I turn around, my eyes connect with Graham's.

Music continues to thump around us, a living, breathing thing. He doesn't look away as he brings his drink to his mouth.

As the lights flash across his eyes, I can't pin down what I see there.

Curiosity.

Intrigue.

Dare I say it…lust?

That can't be right though. Not from him. Not Graham. But the longer we stare each other down, the more convinced I am that there is something there. Something I've never seen from him before.

Bode bumps into me, breaking the connection. By the time I look back, Graham is gone. Disappeared without a trace.

Trying not to be obvious, I scan the small VIP area to see where he went, but he's gone.

Fuck.

What in the world was that?

Graham has been acting different lately, and tonight confirms it.

If only he didn't run away so I could ask him…

What the hell was that look? Because for the rest of the night, it's all I can think about.

The way Graham licked his lips. The way it would feel if they were on me.

"You okay, Noah?" Jasper asks.

"Yeah. I'm good."

"You've been quiet since Graham left."

"Sorry. Just trying to enjoy the night."

And *not* think about Graham's lips on mine. He's straight. It's a nonissue.

Then why is my brain making it an issue?

Chapter Eight

GRAHAM

F uck. Does that ever feel good.

Whosever mouth is on my cock right now, it feels fucking amazing. Peeking one eye open, I see a brown head of hair bobbing up and down on me.

That mouth is fucking delicious.

Warm. Wet.

Resting my arms behind my head, I shut my eyes as they continue working their magic.

It's been too long since I've gotten a blow job like this. Maybe that's why I'm so strung out lately. I just needed to get some action.

"Fuck. That feels good, baby," I whisper.

"Mmm." They purr around the head of my dick.

That voice. It sounds familiar, but with the heat buzzing through me, I'm so close to coming, I don't give it much thought.

Until a warm, solid hand squeezes my balls. It's too strong to be a woman. Propping up on my elbows, I gaze down at the person who is working me over.

Noah.

Oh holy fuck. With one flick of his tongue through my slit, I'm—

"Holy shit!" The mess in my boxers pulls me from sleep as the sheets tangle around my legs. "Holy shit!"

Looking down, my dick is popping out of the hole in my plaid boxer shorts, sticky with cum.

Because I had a sex dream.

And not just any sex dream.

A sex dream starring Noah Fields and his mouth. *His* mouth that made me come harder than I have in a long time.

"Fuck."

Looking at the clock next to my bed, it's half past two.

I kick the sheets off from my feet, then head into my bathroom and turn the shower on.

Straight to ice-cold.

I do not need a repeat of what happened.

Of Noah giving me a blow job.

Fuck. Not something I need to be thinking about because my dick is already taking interest again.

Chucking my messy boxers into my laundry basket, I step under the spray of the shower. Not ice-cold, but lukewarm.

Doing nothing to help my still growing problem.

Fuck.

It's hard to ignore my dick as I rinse off, trying my best to push all thoughts of the dream from my head.

Something like that has never happened to me before.

It's been a weird few weeks. That has to be the reason I had a sex dream about Noah.

Seeing that bartender try to pick him up the other night? Was I jealous? Did I want to be the one picking him up instead?

Fuck.

Stop thinking about it.

But the harder I try not to think about it, the more I end up thinking about it. And it's getting too painful to ignore.

Grabbing some body wash for lube, I take myself in hand and slowly start to jack myself. It's immediate relief.

Picturing someone—anyone but Noah—on their knees for me. Another warm mouth. Another hand playing with my balls just how I like. Another set of eyes staring up at me.

That's it.

Nice and slow.

Just how I like. Driving me wild with that tongue of theirs. But right before I come, it's Noah.

Noah's mouth.

Noah's hand.

Noah's eyes encouraging me to come down his throat.

"Fuck!" I shout, painting my release on the shower wall.

Guilt hangs heavy over me as I make quick work of cleaning up my mess and shutting off the water.

Drying myself off, I wipe off the mirror and study myself.

This has never been me. I've never felt bad about getting off before. Now I'm feeling pretty terrible because I have no idea what I'm doing.

What this means.

I've never been attracted to a man before. Having these feelings swirling around inside my head has to mean something.

What, I don't know.

Tossing the towel into the laundry bin with the rest of the evidence of this weird night, I head back into my room to try and sleep.

Except sleep is elusive. I toss and turn all night trying to shut off my overactive brain. What I'm feeling for him isn't real. It's just a reaction to seeing the bartender hit on him the other night. That has to be the only logical explanation for this.

It's an endless cycle of trying to forget about Noah, then thinking too much about him, and then trying to forget again.

Lather, rinse, repeat.

By the time six o'clock rolls around, I give up and grab some clothes to go for a run. Maybe I can sweat out the new feelings I'm having.

After lacing up my tennis shoes, I head to the kitchen and come to an abrupt halt.

Noah.

Standing shirtless in the kitchen drinking a glass of OJ.

Fuck. Me.

As if things weren't hard enough as it is, there he is. Half-naked. Not knowing the havoc he's wreaking on my emotions.

"Hey." His husky voice, heavy with sleep, startles me.

"Uh. Hi."

"Sorry, did I wake you up?" he asks. "I couldn't sleep."

Fuck. I hope I didn't wake him up with the sound of me coming. To thoughts of him.

"No. Couldn't sleep either. Figured I might as well go for a run."

Noah sets his glass down on the counter, wiping his mouth. I focus on the wall behind him so I don't get distracted.

Seeing those lips wrapped around my cock in my dream was bad enough. Seeing them now? I don't need to relive that image.

"You mind if I go with you? I could work out a few things today on my body."

Fuck. Me.

Again.

Does he realize what he's saying? Or is it just my mind turning everything dirty right now?

I have half a mind to say no. To say screw it and just get back into bed and try to sleep this off.

That's not what comes out.

"Sure."

"Great. Give me a few to change and I'll be right out."

"Take your time."

Noah brushes by me as he heads to his room. I do my best to ignore the smell of him. The laundry-fresh scent of his clings to me. Does funny things to my insides. Has my skin feeling too tight for my body.

I grab a glass from the cabinet and fill it to the brim with water before chugging it down. It does little to help.

Especially when Noah comes back out in a skin-tight Knights tee and shorts that show off his muscular thighs.

Things I shouldn't be noticing.

"Ready?"

"Ready."

I am so not ready for this.

Chapter Nine

GRAHAM

"Holy shit. I can't believe we beat them!" Bode tosses an arm over my shoulders as we hit the button for the elevators. "The Black Diamonds! Sorry, Noah."

My eyes drift to my teammates as we stand in the lobby. With an early trip home, we were given strict instructions to head immediately to our rooms.

Just as well.

With everything going on in my head, I could use a good night's sleep. Being around Noah twenty-four seven has been screwing me up.

Thank God it didn't fuck things up tonight.

I'd hate to think what the guys would think of me if they knew my head wasn't in the game because of a guy. Not that I don't think they'd accept me, but would they really want two guys on the same team dating?

I'm not sure anyone would be ready for that amount of scrutiny.

"Why are you saying sorry to me?" Noah shrugs a shoulder, leaning against the wall by the elevator bank, pulling my attention back to the conversation around me. "Not my team anymore."

"You seemed pretty friendly with a lot of them after the game," Jasper chimes in.

"Can't say hi to guys you've played with for eight years?"

"Was it weird to beat them?" Bode asks as the doors to the elevator open and we all pile in.

Noah shakes his head. "Felt fucking awesome. The Knights beating the best team in the league? Fuck yeah."

I don't care that it was only preseason.

"Hell yeah!" Bode's voice echoes around the small space. Leaning back against the mirrored wall, I press the button to our floor and close my eyes, listening as the guys shoot the shit.

I'm exhausted. Even in the preseason, my body is starting to feel it. Maybe it's because Coach Andrews is pushing us harder than our last coach. He was a fine coach, but he didn't work us as hard as we needed.

It was a hard-fought win tonight, and I'm thankful we were up to the task.

"Our floor." An elbow hits me in the side as I open my eyes to see Noah walking out.

"You sure you guys don't want to come up for a drink?" Jasper asks.

"Aren't you supposed to be keeping everyone in check?" Noah asks, holding the door open as I brush past him.

"One drink won't kill us, eh?"

"Coach might," I tell them as the doors close.

"You don't want to go hang out with them?" Noah asks, reaching into his back pocket and grabbing our room key from his wallet.

"Not tonight."

Shoving my hands in my pockets, I make the short walk to our room that's at the end of the hallway. Usually, we're all on the same floor, but not this trip. Something about a convention being in town.

"Everything okay?" Noah jogs to keep up with me. His tie is loosened at his neck, showing off his Adam's apple.

I shouldn't be noticing these things. I *hate* that I'm noticing these things.

It's Noah, for fuck's sake.

"Tired is all."

Waiting as the click of the door lets us in, I make quick work of changing into shorts and a T-shirt. Having showered at the arena, all I want to do is crash tonight.

But I can't.

My brain is spinning in circles at a million miles an hour. I've had a dry spell this season. Maybe if I go out and meet someone, that'll help shut my brain off.

Or maybe I've just driven myself to exhaustion thinking and worrying about Noah. Because if it's not hockey, it's Noah.

That's it.

Hockey and Noah. Noah and hockey. Not a good headspace for anyone to be in.

"Okay, you're being weird," Noah points out, slapping my thigh as he passes my spot on the bed to go to his, having changed out of his suit.

"Fuck off. No, I'm not."

"Yes, you are. You've been weird for a few weeks now."

"Is it because we're getting along?" I try to deflect.

"You're such a dick." He throws a pillow my way with a laugh, but I grab it and shove it back at him. But the momentum of it sends me crashing into him.

Onto his bed.

It takes us a minute to realize how we're lying together

before the playfulness is sucked from the air. I don't think I've ever been this close to Noah in my entire life.

Those brown eyes of his are full of emotions, flitting through before I can pinpoint even one. But the thing I don't miss?

How his hand closes on my hip. Whether to hold me there or push me away, I don't know. Noah's teeth dig into his bottom lip.

Is he waiting for me to make a move?

Every single thing I want to do to this man flashes through my brain. I want to tug that bottom lip out of his teeth and suck it. See what he tastes like. Feel how strong he is under me. Swallow every gasp as I kiss him.

The emotions in his eyes become clear. I couldn't miss it. Not this close to him.

It's desire. Plain as day.

He wants me.

Fuck.

Fuck.

I shouldn't even be thinking about this. Thinking about what he would taste like. But really, it's all I've been able to think about lately. Since I saw our coach with his husband.

Why couldn't it have been anyone but Noah? Noah complicates things. He's my roommate and teammate. And I hated him up until a few weeks ago.

And he's a *man.* I never thought I'd be attracted to someone of the same sex. Somewhere along the last few weeks, something changed. Maybe if I lived with anyone else, I could be attracted to them.

But I'm not.

It's Noah.

When those brown eyes of his dip down to my lips again, I don't think. I push every thought out of my head and lower myself over him, crushing my lips to his.

There's a moment of hesitation. Whether it's his or mine, I'm not sure.

Because holy shit.

I'm kissing Noah Fields. *A man.*

And nothing about it feels weird at all.

That snaps what limited control I have on reality as Noah wraps his arms around me to deepen the kiss.

It's new and familiar all at the same time, but somehow better than I ever remember. The scruff lining Noah's jaw is rough against mine as he slides his tongue against my lips. I willingly cede control to him.

As our tongues tangle, I fit my body over his. The hard planes there make me want to rip off the sweatshirt he's wearing and run my hands over each and every one of his abs.

Trace them with my tongue.

These thoughts are new and should be overwhelming, but they're not. For some reason, with every stroke of Noah's tongue against mine, it feels more and more normal.

Noah flips us over and changes the angle of our kiss. His knee lodges between my legs. The contact has my cock threatening to jump out of my shorts. Sure, I'd thought of this. The reality? It's even better than I imagined.

My fingers find the hem of Noah's sweatshirt and the warm skin there. Fuck, it feels so good. The rough skin of my palm slips farther under.

It's a high I've never felt, kissing Noah like this. I throw my leg around his hips to pull him closer to me. I want this more than I've ever wanted anything else in my life.

More than hockey.

More than any woman.

And it's just a fucking kiss.

The thought of it progressing past that has me pausing.

Because while this is fucking amazing, the thought of taking this further? I don't know if I'm quite ready for that.

"Shit. We should probably go to bed."

It's like Noah is reading my mind. Or maybe he felt that momentary pause. Either way, I'm grateful for it.

"Right."

Noah sits on the bed next to me, scrubbing a hand over his jaw. "Sorry. I got carried away."

"No." My voice is a little more high-pitched, so I clear it. "I wanted it."

"You did?"

I nod. "Yes."

"Well then,"—Noah leans over, giving me one last kiss—"there's a lot more where that came from."

Chapter Ten

GRAHAM

How much longer can I sit here avoiding the rest of my place?

The minute I get home from practice, I grab something out of the fridge to eat—cold, I might add—and run off to my room.

Because I can't face Noah.

Kissing him has turned my entire world on its axis. I can't look at him without wanting to kiss him again. And I shouldn't want that, right?

Right?

The lights of Nashville are bright in my window as I stare down at the city below me. People coming and going without a care in the world, while my thoughts are trying to weigh me down.

I kissed Noah.

Not only is he my teammate, but we're living together. Albeit temporarily, but we're still living together. Kissing could make things weird.

Well, kissing again could.

And just the thought has my cock stirring in my pants.

Fuck.

Why am I reacting like this to Noah? This has never happened to me before. Ever. Hell, I had a sex dream about him and I wasn't as awkward around him as I am now.

Maybe because I know what it's like to taste him.

Fuck. He tasted so damn good that it's seared itself on my brain.

I always considered myself straight. I've had girlfriends in the past. Ones I was in love with, but those relationships ended. No drama, no fuss. We just fell out of love.

Was it me? Was it this part of me that I didn't know was inside me?

My laptop is burning a hole on my bed. I could easily pull it up and search for some porn to see if this is something fleeting or more. The thought of it makes my skin crawl.

Like I'm using someone to try and figure out something about me. A secret no one but me is privy too.

Fuck. I scrub an anxious hand down my face. I can't keep hiding away in my room. It's not healthy. It's not like I don't see Noah at practice. But there, we're on different lines and I can keep to my end of the ice.

I'm a total coward.

Trying to make a decision, I pull my phone out of my pocket and search the area for a gay bar. This might help the never-ending swirling thoughts in my brain.

Confirm a theory or two I might have about my newfound…curiosity, let's call it.

Finding a bar a safe distance from home and the area, I grab a ball cap and jacket out of my closet before listening at my door. Without hearing any noise, I crack the door before making sure the coast is clear. Darting to the front door, I head out toward the elevator and down to the parking garage.

All without having to see my roommate.

Like I said, a coward.

BRIGHT LIGHTS ARE DANCING on the walls as I tuck my wallet back into my pocket once I'm carded. The heavy beat of a pop anthem pulses through my veins, rocking the entire room around me.

Couples are grinding together on the dance floor. The smell of sweat and sex hangs heavy in the air. And I couldn't look more out of place if I tried.

In a T-shirt, jeans, and hat, I'm wearing more clothes than ninety percent of the people here. It doesn't stop the eyes glancing my way as I cut the fastest route to the bar on the opposite side of the room. Glass shelves line the wall with colors lighting them from above.

Finding a spot near the corner, I flag down the bartender and order a beer. No need for anything stronger when I need to keep my wits about me.

As I sip from the bottle, my eyes dance around the room, from the opposite side of the bar to the guys on the dance floor. People are huddled in groups, talking, laughing, and dancing. It seems like everyone here knows everyone else.

Instead of feeling like an interloper, it gives me a minute to breathe. To get my bearings. Pulling my hat down lower, I sip on my beer, letting the buzz race through me.

Whenever I've come out to bars in the past, I was always trying to pick someone up. It's not that I'm a player by any means. But every now and then, I didn't mind finding someone to slip between the sheets with.

Now, I'm watching. Watching others try and pick people up. Trying to see if this is something that interests me.

If only the guys could see me now.

What would they think of me being here? I know sports are more inclusive than they used to be, but the reaction of the fans that pay money to come to games? I don't want the team to deal with that. I don't want to deal with that.

"Hey, gorgeous." A tall, leggy blond drags his fingers across my shoulders and grabs my attention. "Care to buy me a drink?"

"Shouldn't you be asking to buy me one?" I rest my cheek on my fist and drop my elbow onto the bar.

His dark eyes, rimmed in a sparkly shadow, give a long slow perusal of me. A hunger sits there, like he wants to devour me.

Nothing. I feel absolutely nothing under his stare.

Well, that could answer one question I'm dealing with right now.

"I'm hoping you'll buy me one and then ask me my name. Maybe take me home."

I give him an apologetic smile. "Sorry. Not tonight."

"Hmm. Shame." He grabs a napkin from the pile on the bar and looks around for a pen before jotting a number down. "Call me if you change your mind, handsome."

Sliding the number over to me, he's gone in the blink of an eye.

Huh. I've never had such blatant attention from another guy before. Or have I and I've just ignored it?

Maybe I wasn't ready for this after all. Setting the beer

bottle down, I pull out a twenty, ready to head home when my eyes catch on something across the bar.

Someone.

No, not someone.

Noah.

And the look on his face tells me he's hungry.

For me.

Chapter Eleven

NOAH

Thank God for a day off tomorrow.

There's no such thing as an easy win, but our last two games, we had to fight for every inch of ice gained.

The Knights have now won three games in a row. Something they haven't done in years.

And with it, Coach Andrews gave us the morning off from practice before we leave for a West Coast road trip.

I'm thankful for the day off. Maybe I am getting old, but my entire body hurts and doesn't bounce back like it used to.

As I sip on my beer, the lights of the bar flash around me. A disco ball reflects off the mirrored wall behind the bar as couples dance to the music.

There's one good thing about being in Nashville—always a place to go.

The gay bar that I found when moving here is one of the few places I like to come. I can relax and be myself with very few people, if any, noticing who I am.

Except for the first time, someone does notice me. A

pair of familiar eyes connect with mine. It has my jaw dropping.

Graham?

What in the fuck is he doing here?

It's like I caught him with his hand in the cookie jar. He swallows down the rest of his drink and flees.

Setting my own drink down, I follow him toward the long hallway that leads to the bathrooms. Graham is easy to follow. He sticks out like a sore thumb in a mess of men in too little clothing.

Easily catching up to him, I grab his bicep and pull him into a dark corner near the emergency exit.

"What the hell?" he hisses at me.

"What the hell me? What the hell *you*?" I ask him. Graham's eyes are searching, like he's looking to see if we'll be caught.

If he was worried about being caught, he shouldn't have come out tonight. At least, not here.

"What's it matter to you?"

I rest both hands on the wall on either side of his head. The ball cap he's wearing is pulled down low. Music from the club vibrates through the walls back here.

"Imagine my surprise when I come to my usual haunt and see you on the other side of the bar."

"This is your place?"

I push the brim of Graham's hat up to get a better view of him. Stubble lines his jaw. Cheeks flushed pink. Dark eyes taking me in.

"Yes. And I've never seen you here before. It begs the question, why are you here?" I ask again.

"What, are you the police now? Monitoring my every move?"

I shake my head, boxing Graham in. "Because I want to know why *you're* here."

Graham's brown eyes rake over me in a long, slow sweep. It has the alcohol floating through me, drunk on lust.

When his eyes meet mine, I step closer. Graham's dick is hard in his pants—pressing against my own equally hard cock. I push the hat he's wearing up and off his head so I can look closer at him. See everything he's feeling.

"Because I wanted to see if it was a one-time thing with you or if I liked other men."

"And?"

I drop my hand from the wall to cup his neck. The skin is warm, his pulse fluttering as I brush my thumb over it. It picks up speed with each pass over it.

"For some unknown reason, it seems I only react to you."

It's all I need before I'm crushing my lips to his.

Fuck.

There's a moment of hesitation before Graham returns the kiss, opening his warm mouth to accept my tongue.

I can taste the alcohol he was drinking. Blunt fingers dig into my biceps as we explore each other's mouths. The stubble lining Graham's jaw ignites a need inside me that has gone unfulfilled for too many months.

My mouth is hungry as I take everything he's giving me. I run a hand down the soft cotton of his T-shirt and shove it up to reveal the smooth planes of his abs.

The growl it elicits has me thrusting my leg between his. Graham is fucking shameless as he grinds his hardening cock against my thigh.

Fuck. I want to taste it. To swallow him down and take him to the back of my throat.

"May I?"

I squeeze his cock through his jeans and watch as his

teeth dig in to his bottom lip. Graham nods and watches as I slowly free his cock from his jeans.

"Damn."

Graham is well-endowed. A long, thick cock is nestled in a trimmed patch of dark curls at the base.

"Think you can take it?" he asks, a cocky grin on his face. "I know I'm big."

"Hmm. Are you?" Licking my lips, I take his cock in hand. "Watch me, baby."

Dropping to my knees, I suck him down to the base. I relax my jaw even farther when he thrusts into my mouth, pushing himself down my throat.

"Holy shit!" Graham hisses.

I glance up at him and see his eyes staring down at me. Wagging my brows at him, I put on a show.

I've perfected my deep-throating skills over the years. I'm a fucking master at it. So sliding my mouth over Graham's cock—that is as big as he was implying—feels amazing.

The salty precum drags across my tongue as I move up and down at a frantic pace. I have no clue how long we've been back here, but the last thing either of us needs is to be caught.

That would not earn either of us any favor with the team.

Reaching between his legs, I roll his heavy balls between my hands.

"Oh fuck. *Fuck*. That feels amazing."

I give him back a resounding squeeze, letting him know that I know this.

Pulling off him, I drag my tongue along the vein on the underside of his hard length before flicking it through the slit.

"Are you going to come for me, Graham? Come down my throat like I want you to?"

"You do?" he breathes out.

"Yes." I give his balls another squeeze. "I want every last ounce of your cum in my mouth tonight."

"Oh shit."

Based on the way he jacks his hips into the air, I know he's close. Taking a deep breath, I swallow him down again and don't stop until his long fingers fist tight in my hair and he's emptying himself down my throat.

Fuck.

It feels endless as I hold my nose against the base of his cock and feel his cum drip down the back of my throat.

It's the hottest thing I've experienced in a long time.

Hell, probably the best blow job I've given in years.

With Graham Fisher.

Ignoring that fact, I rock back onto my heels and wipe my mouth on the back of my hand. If it weren't for the wall holding up the man in front of me, he'd be in a puddle on the floor. I don't think I've ever seen anyone look so spent after a blow job.

I reach down and grab his hat, putting it on my own head so we don't leave it here. We don't need to leave any trace of what we've done here. Unless you count the inspiration Graham has now given me for all my own sex dreams.

Yeah, I'm that fucking good.

"That felt—"

"Amazing?" I stand, willing my own erection to go down.

"Fuck you."

"I wouldn't say no to that." I smile at him, waggling my brows at him. Graham looks blissed out, and I fucking love that I did that to him.

Instead of answering me, he fists his hands in my shirt and pulls me in for a long, hard kiss.

I let him control this one. Let him taste his release on my tongue. Strong hands roam up and down my back, grasping my ass and pulling me in close to him.

Cupping his cheek, I slow his pace before pulling off him.

Graham looks well and truly fucked.

Reaching between us, I tuck his semi-hard cock—*the fucker is already hard again after a mind-blowing orgasm*—back into his pants and zip him up.

Giving a gentle pat, I step out of his hold, much to my own regret.

"Where are you going?" he asks.

"You and I have some things to discuss."

"Oh yeah?"

"Yes." Dropping a peck on his cheek, I press my lips to his ears. "I am going to wait for you at home where you cannot avoid me and we can discuss what this means."

Graham looks stunned as I pull back. Stunned and sexy as hell.

Good.

"I'll see you at home."

Chapter Twelve

GRAHAM

For the first time in a long while, I'm excited to be pushing my key into the lock of my condo. To see what is waiting for me on the other side of the door.

Instead of everything I'm feeling threatening to overwhelm me, I want to see Noah. I don't want to avoid him.

Not after what we did in the club.

Fuck.

Thinking about it has my dick getting hard. But now is not the time for that. We need to figure out what we're doing.

Pushing open the door, I'm met with a sight that shouldn't make me as happy as it does.

Noah, with his bare feet kicked up on the coffee table, has a drink in hand. He's still wearing my hat. The lights of Nashville cast him in a soft glow. He gives me a small smile.

As if to say *glad you're not avoiding me again.*

"Took you long enough," Noah says. "I was starting to think you might have some regrets."

Closing the door behind me, I toe off my own shoes and slip out of my coat.

"No regrets."

It's true. No matter how wild and errant the thoughts in my head have been about Noah and my feelings for him, I don't regret what we did.

Not for one single second.

"It just took you that long to get home then?"

I drop down onto the couch beside him, leaving space between the two of us. "Got stuck talking to Mrs. Hannigan."

Noah barks out a laugh. "What is she doing out this late at night?"

"She was coming home from a bridge tournament. Took everyone for their money, she said."

"Of course she did." Noah takes a long swallow of his drink.

Suddenly feeling thirsty myself, I grab the glass from him and take my own sip, pressing my lips to the same spot his just were.

The liquid lingers on his lips. I want to lean over and kiss it off. See what he tastes like again.

Will it be as good as the first time?

Will he taste like my cum?

Will he taste like bourbon *and* my cum?

Fuck. It's a heady thought. But I hold back. I'm not sure what we're doing here. Not yet.

"You wanted to talk about this..." I wave a finger between the two of us as I kick one leg up on the couch and lean back into the cushions.

Noah swirls his drink, turning to rest his arm along the back of the couch. "I have a proposition for you."

"Okay."

My dick perks up, taking an interest in where this conversation *might* be going.

"I'm guessing you feeling what you felt tonight is a new thing for you."

"That would be correct." I try not to blush, feeling embarrassed that Noah is able to pin exactly what I'm thinking and feeling.

"I don't have anyone here, so I'm thinking that maybe we could use each other."

"Use each other how?"

Grabbing the glass again, I take another cooling drink. The bourbon is warm and smooth as it goes down. Instead of helping me, all it does is add liquid fire to my veins. Wanting more. Wanting to agree to whatever Noah is asking of me.

"You want to explore this newfound side of yourself. I could use a friends-with-benefits kind of person. And seeing as how I don't have anyone here in Nashville—"

"Does that mean you have someone elsewhere?" I interrupt.

A sly grin slides across his face. I guess I just showed my hand on whether I'll accept his agreement or not. "Not anymore. I had a guy in Denver. We both knew the score. But I got injured and he met someone, so it ended. No hard feelings."

"So I'll be a someone for you now?" I ask.

Noah nods. "Yes. Mutual orgasms for both. You figure out what you're feeling, we both get off. Works for me if it works for you."

His words are casual, but they mean so much more to me. I don't know if I could explore these newfound feelings if it were with anyone else but Noah. Even in these last few weeks, I feel like we've grown closer.

Neither of us are in the mood to rip each other's throats out.

Maybe our clothes now, but we've put the past behind us.

The future? I'm hoping it's going to involve a lot more of what we did at the club tonight.

"What are you thinking?" Noah throws a leg over my lap and settles onto it. My hands go to his thighs on instinct. Fuck, they feel so good.

I never thought thick, solid muscle would do it for me. But it does.

It already has me wanting to rip Noah's clothes off.

"Why do you want to know?" I ask, staring into his hooded eyes.

Oh yeah. Whatever I'm feeling is mirrored by him too.

"Because whatever you were just thinking had this on your face."

Noah traces his thumb over my bottom lip. Opening my mouth, I suck his thumb into my mouth.

I guess if we're doing this, there's no holding back now. His eyes widen as I feel his cock grow thick between the two of us.

"Thinking about getting to do more of what we did tonight with you."

Noah closes the small distance between the two of us, brushing his lips over the shell of my ear. "Is anything off-limits?"

"No."

I dig my fingers into his thighs, spurring him on.

"Sooo…." he starts.

The warmth of his breath has a shudder racking my body. God, I cannot wait to get naked with this man.

"Roommates with benefits?" I ask, pressing a kiss to the

pounding pulse in his neck. The scruff is rough against my lips.

I fucking love it.

"Yes." Noah rocks against me. "Care to seal it with a hand job?"

"Yes."

There is no hesitation in my voice. All need. All want. For Noah.

Fuck. I no longer have to hide these feelings for him. Instead of shying away, I tip my mouth up, seeking his.

Seeking another kiss that I desperately want.

I swallow Noah's groan as he sinks his fingers into my hair. The way he twists the short strands has me thrusting my hips up to meet his.

Sitting back on his knees, Noah makes a show of undoing his jeans and pulling the zipper down. The black cotton hides what I'm desperate to see. And when he finally reveals it?

My jaw drops.

I've never paid attention to another man's dick before. I never had a reason to. But damn, does Noah have a good cock.

"You like it?"

He gives himself a slow stroke. Now that it's in front of me, all the bravado I was feeling dries up.

"I've never done this before," I confess.

"I know." Noah grabs my hand with his free one and rests it on top of his. "Do what you like. See what comes to you. We'll go as fast or slow as you want."

I don't know how I ever thought that Noah was a cocky asshole. He's already more patient with me than I ever thought he would be.

As I squeeze my hand over his, he guides our motion. I'm staring at our hands as they move up and down his cock. The head of his dick is an angry purple. A small drop of pearly, white liquid sits there.

If I had more balls, I'd lean down and lick it. But right now, I'm good feeling his hand under mine as we move along his thick shaft. Noah's movements guide my own, and slowly but surely, they give me more confidence.

Feeling and seeing the way Noah is reacting to me gives me the boost of confidence I need, so I pull his hand off him and replace it with my own.

It's the first time I've ever touched another man's cock. The warm, soft skin. How hard he is underneath.

So fucking good.

"Just like that." Noah is thrusting his hips up through my fist. "So good, Graham."

Noah's hands clasp behind my neck, and he tilts my chin up to meet him. His lips are gentle as he presses a kiss to my mouth.

But it's too soft for what I want.

"Kiss me like you mean it."

"Then jack me off like you mean it."

A slow smile spreads across my face. "Only if you do it to me too."

Noah matches my smile as he slowly undoes my jeans and pulls my cock out. My rock-hard cock.

"It's good to know you can get it up quickly again."

"When there's the possibility of getting off with you? It's easy."

Noah's mouth crashes against mine in a heated kiss as our fists knock into each other while we jack each other off.

Every time his hand glides over the head of my cock, another loud groan erupts from deep in my chest. It matches the hungry way we're attacking each other's mouths.

Desperate.

Needy.

Sinful.

Kissing Noah Fields might just be the best fucking thing I've ever done in my life. He knows how to kiss. How to make you come alive when his tongue touches yours.

It's not long before the heat and sensation is rippling through me.

Ripping my mouth from his, I mutter, "So close."

"Me too."

Noah's fingers dig into my shoulders as our attention turns to our cocks. His skilled hand twists just right and I'm shooting off like a fountain.

"Fuck!" I yell, throwing my head back on the couch. My movements falter, but when I feel Noah come himself, I look down, watching and seeing the evidence of his attraction to me. Of our attraction to each other.

Sweat clings to my skin as I come down from my high. As my muscles slowly release themselves of all the buildup and tension of coming with this man.

Pushing back, Noah cups my cheek in one hand and pulls my gaze to his.

"No regrets?"

"Not one."

When it comes to this man? I don't think I could regret anything.

Chapter Thirteen

GRAHAM

BODE

Did anyone find out what we're doing tonight?

JASPER

Some painting thing the PR team organized. Coach Andrews told us at practice

DAX

Did you not listen?

BODE

Of course I was listening

NOAH

Then what time does it start?

BODE

7:30?

MARCUS

Starts at 7. Don't be late

BODE

When am I ever late?

GRAHAM

You literally just said the wrong time. You would've shown up late

DAX

You're always late

BODE

One time! I was late one time

NOAH

You're always late for practice

BODE

No I'm not! What is this, gang up on Bode night?

Can't take the heat?

MARCUS

Graham with the zing

NOAH

He learned from the best

BODE

Getting a big head then, Fields

JASPER

Ugh.

DAX

Is it too late to send him back to Denver?

MARCUS

Nah...we don't want to. Not since we're winning

NOAH

See? Greatness

MARCUS

I take back what I said

BODE

I like this. Ganging up on Noah

MARCUS

Painting night starts at 7. Don't be late
(looking at you Bode)

BODE

Fuck you

"Hey. Look who's on time."

Getting out of the car, Bode is walking over to us, a snarky look plastered across his face.

"Had to prove a point to you idiots."

"How many alarms did you have to set to remember to come?" Noah asks him, walking around the car.

"Easy for you to say. Graham is the most punctual person on the team besides Marcus. You have a built-in reminder."

The three of us head toward the small shop set in the strip mall near downtown.

"Maybe you should move in with him."

"Hey!" I interject. "I don't need a revolving door of teammates sleeping with me."

"Sleeping with you?" Bode asks, raising his brows at me.

"Uhh…I meant sleeping in my condo." I try to recover, but do a poor job of it.

Jesus. The last thing I need to do is tell the guys what Noah and I are doing. We just started this thing. I'm not ready for it to be over. I want more. Want to see if these things I'm feeling are real, or if they're just a reaction from being so close to Noah.

"Sorry, Flounder. I'm not bringing all the women into your place. We're too loud."

"Can you show a little bit of respect for women?" Marcus grumbles, coming up behind us, smacking Bode in the head. "It's like I'm surrounded by teenage boys."

"Don't lump me in with him," Noah calls after him as the two of us head into the small shop. "I'm better than that."

The studio the team found for the event is an explosion of color. Paintings of all kinds line the bright white walls. Square tables are set up with two blank easels on each side. Sinks line one wall, and a hat tree holds aprons of various sizes. A small stage sits in the middle of the room with an instructor waiting for all of us.

The four of us find an empty table as Jasper walks over to us, dropping into the seat next to Marcus.

"Look who's on time!" Jasper chirps.

Bode flips him off as Dax takes the empty seat beside him.

"Welcome, everyone," the instructor calls out. It cuts off any further argument from Bode. "We're so happy you could join us tonight."

The older woman has a short gray bob, overalls covered in paint, and wears white low-top sneakers.

"Tonight is going to be very low-key. We've got drinks at the bar for you." A few guys whoop at her comment. "We want you to have fun and relax. Express your creativity."

"Think you can handle that?" I ask Noah, who's in the spot next to me. The side of the table facing the instructor is empty so we have a better view.

"Please. I'll show everyone here up."

"I'd say we should make a bet, but I don't know what that would look like with you."

Noah gives me a quick up and down glance. "I have a few things I could think of."

"Not here," I whisper out of the corner of my mouth. I don't need Noah being more obvious than necessary.

"Then tonight at home."

A shudder racks my body. Noah's words are more of a promise than anything else. One I know he will follow through on.

"Okay. You might be wondering what we're doing tonight. Each of you will be painting your seatmate. When you're done, they will go to the team's auction to help support a local school's music program."

"Who picked that?" Noah asks from next to me.

"I did. Why?" Marcus leans forward, looking over at Noah. "You have a problem supporting kids learning music?"

Noah throws his hands up in defense. "No. I like it. I just didn't know who was in charge of that kind of thing with the team."

Marcus scrubs a hand over his face. "Sorry, Strawberry. The girls are sick and I'm tired."

Noah cuts his eyes from Marcus to throw a glare my way. "Where in the hell did you hear that name?"

"Flounder. Why?"

I can't help the smirk that threatens to take over my entire face as the instructor continues with her instructions.

"Supplies are on the back wall. Grab whatever paint you need, and your brushes and water are in between your stations."

"I thought I was going to shake that nickname here," Noah grumbles.

"What? I can't share a nickname for you?" I cross my

arms and spin around in my stool, taking in the guy next to me.

"Aww. Poor baby." Marcus ruffles his hair as he goes to grab his paint supplies. "Now that's the only thing we're going to call you."

"I could kill Nick," Noah mutters to himself.

"But then who would I get to tell me all the good stuff on you?" I bat my eyelashes at him. "I missed a lot when you were in Denver."

"I'm going to have a conversation with ol' Nicky." Noah ignores me.

"I'll make sure I get the scoop then before you get to him."

Pulling out my phone, I pretend like I'm going to text him when Noah makes a grab for my phone.

"I wouldn't do that if I were you."

"Why not?"

Noah looks around, and when he's sure no one is listening, he mutters, "Because otherwise I won't do all the things I'm planning on doing to you tonight."

"You play dirty."

"I'll get the paint." Noah ignores me, whistling as he heads toward the paint station to get what we need. Damn. He really does know what he's doing. The promise of what the night holds is too good to be true.

But I shouldn't be thinking about that right now. Definitely not something I should be thinking about in mixed company.

"You have two hours. I'll be around to help as needed, but in the meantime, have fun with this. Let your artistic abilities loose!"

"Do you even have an artistic bone in your body?" Jasper asks Bode, who is now sitting across from him.

"I've got one bone that does the job. I don't need to be creative."

"Gross, man!" All of us chide him from our spots around him.

"Seriously. How you don't have an STI at this point is mind-boggling." Marcus shakes his head from next to me before dabbing his paintbrush in a blue color and starting his work of painting Jasper.

"Aren't you glad you're here?" I ask Noah. Based on the look of concentration on his face, he's already hard at work painting me.

Not to be outdone by him, I grab my own paintbrush and start in on my canvas. The last time I painted had to be in kindergarten with finger paints.

By the time I was old enough to express interest in anything, I was already playing hockey. If I had any creativeness inside me, I put it all on the ice.

Swirling the paints on my tray together, I study Noah with more concentration than this exercise calls for.

But it's an easy excuse to look at him.

Because Noah Fields is quite possibly one of the sexiest people I've ever laid eyes on.

The dark brown hair that's always falling into his even darker brown eyes.

The way his lips curl up into a playful smile.

The strong set of his jaw.

And that's only the tip of the iceberg.

Trying to stop my head from going down the "why is Noah sexy" road, I turn my focus back to the canvas in front of me and can't help but laugh.

"What?" Noah chimes in from across the table. "Do I look sexy as hell?"

Marcus peers over and lets out a belly laugh. "You do know that he isn't an alien, right?"

"Shit."

In letting my thoughts run wild about the man I'm supposed to be painting, I mixed the paint wrong, with Noah's skin being green and his hair being a light orange color.

"You really should be paying more attention," Jasper agrees. "I don't know if anyone would want to buy that. It'd give kids nightmares."

"You're an asshole." I shove him back over to where his own canvas is. "Yours isn't much better."

Marcus looks like he has one eye that overtakes his entire head. A small line looks like it's supposed to be his mouth, but you can't really tell.

"Would you like a new canvas?" the instructor asks as she comes around. Her face is one of shock as she takes in the canvases at our table. "You still have enough time to start over."

"Uhh, sure. I guess so," I tell her.

"We can dispose of this if you'd like."

"No!" Noah chimes in. "I want to keep it."

"You really want to keep this?" I ask him. I'm starting to question this man's sanity.

"I want to hang it in the living room when we get home. It's hilarious."

"Fuck off, you asshole."

"Wouldn't you like that." He waggles his eyebrows at me.

"How about we hang this in the locker room? We could use it for darts," Jasper tells us. "Rough up this guy's mug."

"Not enough darts in the world to do that," Noah quips.

The instructor's head is swiveling around between all of us, looking at us like we've lost our minds. I don't think she knew what she signed up for when she agreed to have the Knights here for a little team bonding and PR.

"Alright. Get a new canvas and start over, Graham. Go back to your own paintings." Marcus doesn't even have to look at us to get us into gear.

I guess that's why we've named him captain for the last two years.

Noah's eyes are sparkling from beside me.

Because I know what the rest of the night holds.

And I can't fucking wait.

Chapter Fourteen

GRAHAM

Tension fills the elevator. Noah is so damn close to me that I'm going out of my mind with need. One brush of his elbow against mine and I might come.

Time slows as we pass each floor.

Why the hell are we on the second to top floor?

Out of the corner of my eye, Noah's eyes are raking me up and down. Each slide of his eyes over me has my skin feeling too tight for my body. I want to be naked with Noah. To feel his eyes on me without clothes or the empty space of an elevator between us.

Fuck. The thought of it has me trying to rearrange the growing erection in my jeans.

When the elevator finally beeps, I'm bursting out into the hallway with a fervor that has Noah laughing behind me.

"Anxious?"

"Ready."

This time, Noah presses a hand against my chest and pushes me back toward our front door. "Then get your ass inside."

I spin to open the door as Noah crowds in behind me. My hands are nervous as I push the key inside the lock and shoulder it open.

The entire place is dark except for the lone light on above the oven. City lights blink in through the windows as Noah shuts the door behind us and pulls me in the direction of his room.

His large hand is warm, sending sparks shooting through me. Now that we're in Noah's room, nerves are starting to swarm.

I haven't been in here since Noah moved in. It's sparsely decorated—one nightstand next to a king bed with plain navy sheets and a gray comforter. Clothes are spewing out of the laundry basket. It shouldn't have me laughing, but it does.

"Do you ever clean up?" I ask Noah as he stalks toward me.

He raises a brow at me. "That's what you're thinking about right now?"

Noah closes the bedroom door behind me and crowds me against it. On instinct, my hands fly to his waist and pull him to me. Noah's hard cock lines up against mine. "Among other things."

"What other things?" Noah drags his nose along my neck. Digging my fingertips into his side, I try to keep my thoughts from spiraling.

"How I want to see you naked."

"Mm-hmm." Noah nibbles on the hollow under my Adam's apple. "Keep going."

Holy fuck, does that ever feel good.

"I wouldn't mind another blow job from you."

Noah tugs my earlobe between his teeth before licking the sting away. "You like my mouth on you?"

"So fucking much."

"Good. What else?"

Shoving his hands up and under my shirt, he tugs it off me and throws it behind him. His fingertips brush against my nipples, and it has my cock punching a hard pattern against my jeans zipper.

"That. I like that."

"Yeah?" Noah leans closer and flicks the hard nub with the tip of his tongue. "How about that?"

"Fuck." I bite out. "Do that again."

This time, Noah tugs my nipple between his teeth and I arch against him. Ignoring me, Noah presses hot, open-mouthed kisses all over my chest.

How can this man be driving me so wild with need and lust? I'm strung out in a way I've never felt before, and I've only had his mouth on my chest. The thought of having sex with him? Damn. It has my mouth watering.

"May I?" Noah is on his knees, eyes dark as he stares up at me with his hand on my belt.

"Yes. God, yes."

The bastard doesn't do anything to put me out of my misery. Or pain, as it may be. My dick is so fucking hard, it's ready to bust out of my pants, but Noah is brushing his fingertips against the hard material and not doing anything else.

"Fuck me."

Noah nips at my hip bone. "Patience, Graham."

My name on Noah's lips has me sifting my fingers through his hair and turning his gaze toward me. I bend over and press my own mouth to the corner of his. "I'm running out of it. I want your mouth on my cock. Now."

Noah steals a kiss, his tongue greedily taking what he wants. What I'm willingly giving him. Noah on his knees for me holds all the power. But it doesn't mean I'm not going to make him work for it.

The teasing nips and bites are too much for me. I want to be shoving my cock in that mouth of his and feeling that wet heat again.

"Well, with an argument like that, how can I keep you waiting?"

The snick of the zipper being dragged down echoes around the room. Noah shoves my jeans down my legs before untying my shoes and pulling them off. When his hands drift back up my legs to my briefs, he pulls them down and tucks the band under my balls.

The hungry look on Noah's face has me pushing my dick into his face. He grabs it, rubbing his thumb through the slit at the top.

"You really like my mouth on your cock, don't you?"

"Yes," I groan.

Noah's tongue swipes out to taste the pearl of precum that sits there. It's like that one lick of his tongue sets off something in Noah. Gone is the patient man who is taking his time with me. In his place is a man with a hunger in his eyes.

Noah sucks me down in one swallow, and it brings me back to that night in the bar. Strong fingers play with my balls, and if I didn't want to wait and come when this man is fucking me—or me him—I would keep going. Keep bumping my cock toward the back of his throat as his fingers stroke the tender skin of my taint.

"Fuck. How are you so damn good at this?" I mutter, thrusting into his mouth. "So fucking good."

Noah's eyes are fucking sparkling as he stares up at me. The slight tilt to the corner of his mouth tells me he knows exactly what he's doing to me. Noah pulls off me with a wet pop and stands. "I know."

His lips are swollen as he grabs the neck of his shirt and whips it off. Perfectly sculpted muscles are ripe for my perusal. I want to lick each ab of his. See if he likes his nipples being played with as much as I do.

It's like my own personal striptease as Noah steps out of his jeans and remains in only his boxers.

"Aren't you going to take it all off for me?"

I'm aching to see his dick. Maybe it'll finally catch up to me that I'm about to have sex with a man when I do see it, but right now, all the lust and pleasure is clouding out every other thought in my head.

"Why don't you do it for me?"

Pushing off the wall, I kick off my boxer briefs and give myself a hard stroke as I close the distance between the two of us. Noah's eyes rake over my now naked body.

There's that sense of power again. The tip of his cock is peeking out of his boxers, and it's a heady sensation that I can make him—*Noah*—feel like this.

Hooking my thumbs into the band of his red plaid boxers, I push them down his thighs and sink to the floor as I tap his foot to take them off.

I don't know if I would describe a dick as pretty, but damn, does Noah have a pretty dick. The head is an angry purple with a vein running along the underside of his long, thin shaft.

I lick my lips as the first fingers of fear take hold.

"Are you just going to stare at it?"

Noah takes hold of the base, stroking it right in front of my face. I want to lick the tip. To see how he tastes.

Salty? Sweet?

A strong hand grasps my chin and tilts my vision to his. "What's wrong? Having second thoughts?"

The tenderness in his voice has me shaking my head.

"I just…I want it to be good for you."

Noah's thumb brushes my bottom lip and I open,

sucking the tip in. "Do what you like. I'll tell you if you do something I don't like."

I nod and swipe my tongue along the head. It's a different taste than I expected. My movements are hesitant. Unsure. But with each moan of Noah's, it spurs me on.

I curl my tongue under the head and that has him thrusting in my mouth. "Do that. More of that."

Glancing up at him, I see his head is thrown back in pleasure. Sucking in a breath through my nose, I do my best to work him over like he did me. My own cock is aching with need as Noah thrusts into my mouth, causing me to choke around him.

"Shit. Sorry."

Noah tries to pull back, but I don't let him. Grabbing hold of his delicious ass, I keep him in my mouth. It might be sloppy and hurried, but the whispered words of encouragement tell me that Noah is liking this.

No. *Loving* this.

Noah pulls out of my mouth and hooks his arms under mine to pull me up. He walks us backward toward the bed as his lips seek mine out.

Our combined taste lingers there. I push him back on the bed and settle my weight on top of his. The brush of his cock against mine has me rutting against him, tearing my lips from his as Noah wraps his hands around the two of us.

"How do you want to do this, Graham?" Noah asks.

"What do you mean?"

"Top? Bottom?"

"Umm…"

"I'm vers," Noah clarifies, "so do you want to fuck me?"

I lick my lips at the thought of filling Noah. My cock twitches and Noah sees it.

"You like that idea?" Noah asks. "Fucking me?"

"Right now? Yes."

"Then let's do it."

Noah reaches over to the nightstand and fishes around, pulling out a bottle of lube and a strip of condoms.

"How do I do this?" I rock back onto my heels as Noah sets his feet down and opens himself up to me. My gaze doesn't leave his hand as he opens the lube and rubs it between his fingers before pressing one finger against the pucker of his ass.

I bite down on my bottom lip as he slowly works the long, thick digit in and out of himself, then watch as he inserts two.

Grabbing the lube, I pour more than is necessary on my hand and work one in as he's slowly stretching himself.

Emotions play out on his face as he pulls his fingers out and I push two back in.

"Like that. That's good."

I take my time, listening as Noah encourages me.

"I'm good. I'm ready."

"Yeah?"

"Yeah." Sweat clings to Noah's brow as I reach for the condoms. Noah halts me from rolling it down my length, and I want to weep because I am about ready to explode.

"You know…" Noah starts.

"What?"

"I haven't been with any guys since I got all my tests done with the team and I'm on PReP."

"I am too," I tell him.

"You are?"

I nod, running a hand down his side. The strong muscles flex under my touch. I like seeing the reaction I bring out in him. "I am. I did some research after the club and figured it'd be a good thing to start."

"So you're saying no condoms?"

"If you're okay with it, yes. My latest tests were all negative."

The sly grin spreads across Noah's face before his lips crash down on mine. His stubble brushes against my cheeks and I love the feel of it. How Noah tastes.

I never thought I would be this tied up over someone. Over *a man*.

But here I am. On the edge of the abyss with the man who drives me crazy.

"Flip over."

I do as instructed and watch as he settles over me. Strong thighs sit on either side of me as he takes me in hand and slowly sinks down.

And holy fuck.

I don't think I've ever felt anything so fucking good in my life. The way his ass is squeezing me? I have to think of every non-sexy thing I can think of so I don't come immediately. Noah drops to his elbows on either side of my face.

"Do you know how good you feel?" Noah shifts his hips and it has me pushing my dick up into him.

I run my hands up his legs, loving how the hair feels under my calloused palms. "Not as good as you."

"Not possible."

His lips hover over mine as we start moving together in tandem. We're sharing the same air. Drinking each other in as every single cell in my body converges to the point where I'm inside of Noah.

Every feeling is etched on his face as I pump my hips harder and faster into him.

I take his dick in hand, which is making a mess of his chest, and jack him off. "C'mon, Noah."

My voice is gruff as my movements become sloppy. I'm out of my mind with need.

Noah drops his forehead to mine. "I want you to come first. I want to feel you exploding inside of me. Feel your cum dripping out of my ass."

"Holy fuck!" I shout.

That's all I needed to hear. The fissure of ecstasy starts in my chest, spreading through my limbs until it explodes out of me into a million tiny pieces.

My grip on Noah's cock falters as he tightens his hand around mine. Only a few more pumps and ropes of cum are spreading across my chest. Noah's face as he orgasms —which seems endless—twists in pleasure as he throws his head back.

Fuck. Noah looks so damn sexy, it has my cock twitching once again before he collapses on top of me.

"Fuck, Graham. That was…incredible."

I drag a finger down the notches in Noah's spine as we both try to come back down to earth.

How do I tell Noah that might have been one of the greatest sexual experiences I've ever had? I don't know if I'm ready to deal with that level of cockiness from this man.

"I need to catch my breath, but—"

"You want to do that again?" Noah asks, slipping off of me.

"All fucking night."

Chapter Fifteen

NOAH

"What's it going to take for you to see your old man?" Dad asks.

"You know better than anyone what a professional athlete's schedule looks like," I tell him, shouldering open the front door after practice. Graham is right behind me and brushes by me.

My entire body reacts at the mere closeness of him. It shouldn't. It's too early for this. I'm not the kind to have these reactions. I keep things casual. It's better with my crazy life. Then why am I reacting to Graham?

It can't just be because the sex is so good.

Not good. Fucking great. Better than anything else I've had, and it's all with a guy who is still trying to figure things out.

"Are you listening to me?" Dad asks, breaking me out of my thoughts.

"Sorry, what?"

"We'll be in town Sunday for the football game. Want us to get you tickets to come with us?"

"Sure."

"Bring Graham too. I know Knox will want to see him."

I laugh. "You act like we never call or see you. I saw you like two months ago."

Dad sighs over the phone as Graham comes back into the kitchen after dropping off his bags. He's lost his sweatshirt and is only in a pair of low-slung sweats.

Fuck. Me.

"We'll see you Sunday, okay?"

"See you then. Bye."

"Bye—"

I hang up the phone before I can say anything that might give away what I'm feeling.

"Are you trying to drive me crazy?" I growl at Graham, who has now bent over and is grabbing something from inside the fridge.

"Wasn't trying to, no."

When he turns around and leans against the counter, the cocky smile on his face tells me his words are a lie.

That is exactly what he wanted to do. The man standing in front of me is infuriating. Because he knows he can drive me wild with need.

Fuck. I need to shut down this line of thinking.

"Who was on the phone?"

Graham does it for me. Leaning against the opposite counter, I cross my legs, mirroring Graham's position. "My dad."

"How are your parents?"

I nod my head. "Good. Our dads will be in town this week."

Graham smiles at me. "My mom texted me earlier this week that they would be."

"Didn't care to share that nugget of information?"

I watch as Graham sips his water, swallowing it down,

mesmerized by his throat. Again, he knows it too by the look on his face.

"I only assumed they told you."

I scoff. "Well, I just found out. And we were invited to go to the game with them."

"We were?"

I nod. "It seems more like a demand, really."

"Are you demanding that I go with you?" Graham asks.

"Not demanding. I was hoping you'd want to come with me of your own free will."

Graham closes the distance between us and drops his hands on either side of my hips. I'm completely enveloped in his space.

"What, like a date?" Graham asks.

"Well, a non-date date."

"I have half a mind to say no because if this is you asking, no wonder you haven't had a serious relationship."

"Ouch." I laugh. "Below the belt."

"If the shoe fits…"

"Hey!" I smack his muscular chest. He doesn't flinch. "It's not like you're looking for a relationship."

Something flashes across his face, but it's gone before I can pin it down. Whatever he's feeling, he keeps to himself.

"It doesn't mean we can't go to the game together."

"You want to?"

"As a non-date date?" Graham asks, slowly nodding his head. "I wouldn't mind that."

"Good." I sink down to my knees. "Now I would like to do something that I don't think you'll mind either."

"I CAN'T TELL you the last time I've been to a football game," I tell Graham as we take the elevator up to the suites.

"Really? I know it's all hockey all the time, but really?"

"Really."

The elevator doors open, and we're met with masses of people, even on the suite level. With the game close to starting, we fight our way to the suite where our families are.

"I don't have as much invested in the game," I say.

"I guess I wouldn't have either if my mom hadn't coached the team."

"Hopefully they'll win today."

Graham leans over, moving out of the way of approaching fans. "Don't let anyone hear you say that too loudly."

I bump his elbow with mine. "Even if we play for the Knights, I'm not adopting their football team."

Nashville's football team isn't the best, but they've been doing better in recent years. With some solid coaching, they could be a top contender.

Hopefully the same thing can be said for the Knights.

A few people recognize us as we head down the hall toward the suite our family is in. Pictures of the team and Nashville line the walls. The crowd in the stands can be heard even from here.

Finding the right suite, I push the door open and we're met with a wall of sound, laughter and joking from the guys within.

It's a familiar sight. All of them standing around, talking and giving each other a hard time. Until now, I didn't realize how much I missed it.

Back in Denver, I saw them a lot more than I realized.

I didn't make it to a lot of football games, but these guys have always been in my life.

"My own son, as I live and breathe." Dad sets his drink down and walks over to me to pull me in for a hug. "I'm glad to see you're still alive, even if you can't call your own parents."

"Dad," I groan, returning the hug. "You know how busy I've been."

"Too busy to call your old man?" He ruffles my hair.

"Jackson, leave him alone," Uncle Alex tells him. "He's been busy adapting to a new team."

"See? At least someone gets it," I agree.

"You've been looking good as a team," Uncle Colin tells us. "Maybe it's all down to Noah's work ethic."

"Hey!" Graham cuts in. "I resent that."

"I'm kidding." Colin laughs.

"I've told you," Knox interjects, "to never listen to what Colin says."

"Rude!" Colin acts affronted, but knowing him, he isn't. He's been like this for as long as I've known him.

It's the familiarity of being with everyone that I love that makes me happy Graham and I came on this "non-date date."

Crowd noise explodes around us as boos echo in the space with Denver running onto the field. I fight the smile because no matter where I live, Denver will always be my football team.

"Think Denver will win?" Graham asks as he sidles up next to me.

"They better. It's the only game I'm going to, and I don't want to be bad luck for them."

Graham laughs. "You know you shouldn't believe in that."

"I don't. At least, not for us."

"Ah. How big of you. You can be bad luck for Denver but not for the Knights."

I eye Graham. "Well, if we go by that logic, I think we're going to need to start getting off before games."

He chokes over his beer. "I'm sorry, what?"

"The other day." I turn to face the field as the captains head out to the field for the coin toss. "I'm pretty sure I gave you a blow job before the game and we won."

"Is this really the conversation we should be having right now?" Graham hisses from the corner of his mouth.

I shrug a shoulder as I spin from my spot and head toward the rows of seats that overlook the field.

"No. But I like seeing you blush," I whisper so only he can hear me.

Damn. He really makes it easy to make him blush. Hell, so far, everything about being with Graham is easy.

Everyone settles into their seats as the game starts. Graham moves into the front row next to his dad, doing a pointed job of ignoring me.

I'll get him back for that later tonight.

The game goes by in a blink with Denver taking a fast lead and not letting up. Heading back into the suite to get more food, my eyes keep glancing over to where Graham is watching the game with his dad. It's weird. We're here together, but not together.

That seems to be what our relationship boils down to. If you can call what we're doing a relationship.

I've never really had one before. Why am I wanting to start one with Graham? Everything he's feeling is new. He's not even out. I shouldn't be considering doing this thing with the man in question.

The man who is now peering over his shoulder and smiling at me.

It's messing with my head.

"You know." Dad comes up and stands next to me. We're facing the field as the teams are lining up for the start of the fourth quarter. "You seem happier here."

"Really?" I turn to face him now.

He nods. When he looks at me, it's like I'm staring into a mirror of what I'll look like when I'm his age.

"I don't think it's just hockey. You had hockey in Denver. It's something else."

"This feels like a good place to be."

It's all I can give. I can't tell him that Graham and I are…roommates with benefits?

I wish I could have a clear head to figure this out. Because when Graham walks by me, and I catch the smallest whiff of his cologne, it casts a lusty fog over me.

Damn it.

I know what I signed up for, but I want more with Graham. If only there was a way to get it.

Chapter Sixteen

"Does it really matter what we watch?" Noah asks, strutting into the bedroom from the bathroom. "Are we really going to be paying attention to it?"

The channels flip by until I find a hockey game to settle on.

"Last time, you picked a horror movie that gave me nightmares for a week." I chuck the remote at him and he throws an arm up to dodge it.

"I told you, I didn't know it was a horror movie. Otherwise I would have picked something more in line with your sensibilities."

I wish I'd waited to throw the remote at him now.

"You're a dick."

"You like it."

"In your dreams, Fields."

Standing between our beds, Noah stares me down as he grabs the back of his shirt and pulls it off. The cocky fucker throws it at me.

"You dream about all this?"

Seeing his hand move in my peripheral vision, I

ignore its path. Absolutely ignoring as it trails up and over his well-defined pecs and the abs that are on full display.

"You wish."

Standing up, I get close to him and pull my own T-shirt off. Noah's eyes don't leave mine, but I can see the obvious desire there. It mirrors my own.

It's getting harder and harder to hide my want and need for this man.

Noah smirks before I hear the crinkle of a bag and icy coldness is thrust into my chest. "Here."

Looking down, I grab the pint of strawberry froyo that we picked up on our way to the room. And to think, only a few months ago, I found Noah Fields to be one of the most annoying guys on the planet.

Now he's annoying for an entirely different reason. Just for looking so damn sexy as he settles onto his bed and turns his eyes to the game.

I follow suit and rest my back against the firm, wooden headboard of the hotel bed. We're playing Vancouver tomorrow and flew in after our game with Dallas. At this point in my career, all the rooms are starting to blend together—the same wall art focusing on whatever city we're in. Cheap and itchy bedspreads. A bathroom too small for two oversized hockey players.

Not that I'd know about that last one. But now that the thought is there, I wouldn't mind seeing if the two of us can fit.

Noah's shouts at the TV interrupt my thoughts. I should be watching the game—assessing our opponents and finding their weaknesses—but I just can't bring myself to care.

Because lying here in the hotel room brings back one of my favorite memories from when I was a kid. "You know, I always thought things like this were fun when I was a kid."

"Really?" he asks from his spot on the other bed.

I nod, taking another bite of the sweet treat I allow myself every now and then.

"I remember one time my dad took me to visit my mom where the team was playing. I couldn't tell you why we went, but I remember surprising her and getting to stay up late and eat ice cream and watch movies."

Noah laughs. "Isn't that what every kid. wanted? Staying up late and eating ice cream?"

"I guess so. After that, we did it maybe once a year when mom was traveling. Before I started playing hockey."

"Your mom is still a badass," Noah tells me. "I remember I wanted to be like her when I was little."

"You did?"

"Well, after I won a few Super Bowls because I was the greatest kicker to ever play the game."

I laugh. "Of course you would think that."

"Hey, we both somehow ended up playing hockey with football stars for dads."

"I know why I started playing hockey," I mumble.

"You wanted to be cool like me, right?"

"I mean, didn't we all?"

Noah stabs his spoon into his chocolate yogurt and sets it on the nightstand. "Wait, seriously?"

I look down at the pink frozen yogurt and take another bite. "I mean, you started playing and then everyone else was. I thought it'd make me cool like you. Make you like me."

"I don't know where we started hating each other, but I'm glad we're not there anymore."

"Me too," I agree.

The blue light of the TV casts Noah in a cool glow.

He's spread out in only a pair of black gym shorts. Noah shifts so his eyes are focused on the TV, giving me time to study him. I never thought I'd be attracted to a man.

When I found him in that club, the minute my eyes connected with his, I knew.

It's him.

I don't want to explore things with other men. I just want Noah. It's made it hard for me to worry about if this feels wrong or not. Every time I'm with him, it feels more and more right.

I smile down into the quickly softening yogurt, swirling it around with my spoon. Jesus, I feel like I have a crush.

"You're thinking pretty hard over there." Noah's voice interrupts my thoughts.

"Hmm?"

My eyes meet his as he stares back at me. He's flipped onto his side, yogurt cup sitting empty on the nightstand between us.

"You can't be that excited about ice cream."

"Technically froyo," I throw back at him.

Noah stands, closing the short distance between the beds in one stride before taking my froyo container and setting it next to his. He throws one leg over my lap and settles down on top of me.

Noah's mere presence is overwhelming in the best way. Everything we've done has been at my pace. Sure, he likes to be the one in charge in the bedroom, but from the minute this thing started between us, he put me at ease.

I think it's why I'm so addicted to him.

To everything we're doing together.

"Are we really going to discuss the merits of ice cream versus froyo?" Noah asks, pulling me down the bed so I'm flat on my back.

"Did you have something else in mind?"

I drag my hands down his chest, rubbing my thumbs over his nipples.

"Maybe we could take off some more clothes?"

Noah snaps the band of my shorts, and it has me squirming underneath him.

"I want you to fuck me," I blurt out in a rush.

"Okay?" Noah states, more like a question, rocking back ever so slightly.

I sit up, my hard cock sagging ever so slightly. "I mean, I really liked fucking you, but…"

"But what?" Noah asks.

It feels embarrassing to tell Noah this, but if I can't tell him, who can I tell?

"I've been experimenting."

"Oh yeah?"

This has Noah slotting himself between my legs and pushing me back down onto the bed.

"Promise you won't make fun of me?"

"When have I ever made fun of you?"

"Seriously?" I ask him.

He laughs, his warm breath ghosting over my lips.

"Okay, fine. But I promise. I won't make fun of you."

"I bought a vibrator. Wanted to see what that was all about."

A heated gaze washes over Noah's face. "You bought a vibrator and didn't think to tell me?"

"I thought you'd be mad."

Noah presses the corner of his mouth against mine. I can taste the chocolate there.

"Only that you didn't let me watch you use it. Fuck, Graham. You know we're going to have to use this when we get home, right?"

"Think you can use your dick until then?"

Noah slams his mouth down over mine, and fuck me.

I'm ready to let this man devour me as I spin us so I'm on top of him. The strength and power he wields is such a turn-on.

I rock my hips into his. The brief contact has my cock plumping up in my shorts.

As our kisses intensify, Noah's hand drifts beneath the hem of my shorts and finds my dick. Dropping onto my elbows, my gaze follows his hand as he frees me from the cloth prison of my shorts.

Even after only being together a few times, Noah knows exactly what I like. Exactly what to do to get me off. I love seeing how his hand can fit around the entire girth of my dick.

"You're really good at this."

"You have a really good dick for it."

Noah smirks at me as he spits into his hand to get a better grip. I pump my hips into his fist, getting closer and closer to getting off.

"I'm getting close," I hiss.

Noah smirks before pushing me off him. "Get on your back."

Following his instructions, I do as he asks. Noah hops off the bed to go to his bag and grab supplies. Shucking off my shorts, I give my cock a squeeze to stave off my impending release.

When Noah turns around, I'm practically drooling at the look in his eyes.

"Spread your legs."

"Are you always this bossy?"

"When I get to fuck you? Yes."

Doing as Noah says, I widen my legs for him. He doesn't say anything as he kneels between my legs. Noah's hands trail up and down my thighs. The contact has heat pooling in my groin. My cock is leaking all over my stomach.

"If you want to stop, just tell me."

"Okay."

"I mean it." Noah drags a finger down my chest, ignoring my cock and moving it around my balls. Anticipation grows as his finger slides down my taint and traces my puckered hole. But before he can do much of anything, he's pulling back.

"What—" Bending over, Noah's mouth replaces his fingers. His tongue traces the hole and —"holy fuck!"

I practically fly off the bed as Noah's tongue peppers my ass with attention. I don't know if I've ever felt anything so good. When it pushes inside, I melt.

The fervor with which Noah is eating my ass has me ready to come. I have to squeeze my dick to hold it off. Based on the look Noah is giving me, he knows it.

Pulling back, Noah has a cocky grin on his face. "You like that?"

"You know I do."

"I think you'll like it more when I fuck you." Noah lubes up his fingers before pushing one inside. "Just breathe and push against me."

I do as he says, relaxing as he pushes past that first ring of muscle. It's different from the vibrator but also the same in that it's not an entirely unwelcome feeling.

I try not to let the burn overwhelm me and allow the other sensations to take over. As he continues stretching me, it feels better and better with each finger he adds.

"I'm ready."

Noah pulls his fingers out and lies down on top of me. The first flutter of nerves bubble up in my stomach as he lines himself up with my hole.

Sensing my nerves, Noah kisses me as he pushes an

inch or so inside. His mouth on mine is the distraction I need as he continues pushing into me. My fingers dig into his back, anchoring me to him.

When he's fully seated inside me, Noah runs a hand up and down my side in a tender way.

"You doing okay?"

"Yeah."

Aside from the slight burn, it's not as bad as I thought.

"Tell me when you're ready."

Taking another moment, I pull Noah's lips down to mine. The slow, easy kiss helps to distract me. And with each stroke of his tongue against mine, my dick is perking up between us.

"I'm ready."

Noah's pace starts off slow and steady. Until he hits my prostate.

"Holy fuck! Oh fuck."

"You like that?"

"God, yes."

Noah keeps thrusting. Keeps pegging that same spot that has cum leaking all over my stomach. Noah drags a finger through the sticky substance and sucks it into his mouth. "Fucking delicious."

The look on his face has me coming harder than I ever have in my life.

"Fuck! Fuck, fuck, fuck!"

It seems endless. Cum spurts out of my cock all over my chest.

"Yessss." Noah's neck strains as he comes. Watching the way his body releases that tension has one last rope of cum coming out of me before Noah collapses on top of me.

We're a hot and sticky mess. Slipping out, there's a slight sting, but it's tempered by the sight of Noah walking to the bathroom. He comes back into the room with a washcloth in hand.

Noah's touch is tender as he wipes the cum off me and drops the washcloth onto the floor.

"How do you feel?" Noah lies on his back next to me, linking his hand with mine.

"I know you said you're vers…"

"Yeah?"

Noah turns his head ever so slightly to face me. He's blissed out, cheeks pink after his orgasm. Fuck is it ever sexy.

"I'm thinking I might not be."

"You want to bottom?"

I nod. "Is that okay?"

Noah rolls to his side, resting his head on his elbow.

"Getting to fuck you, Graham? I can't think of anything better."

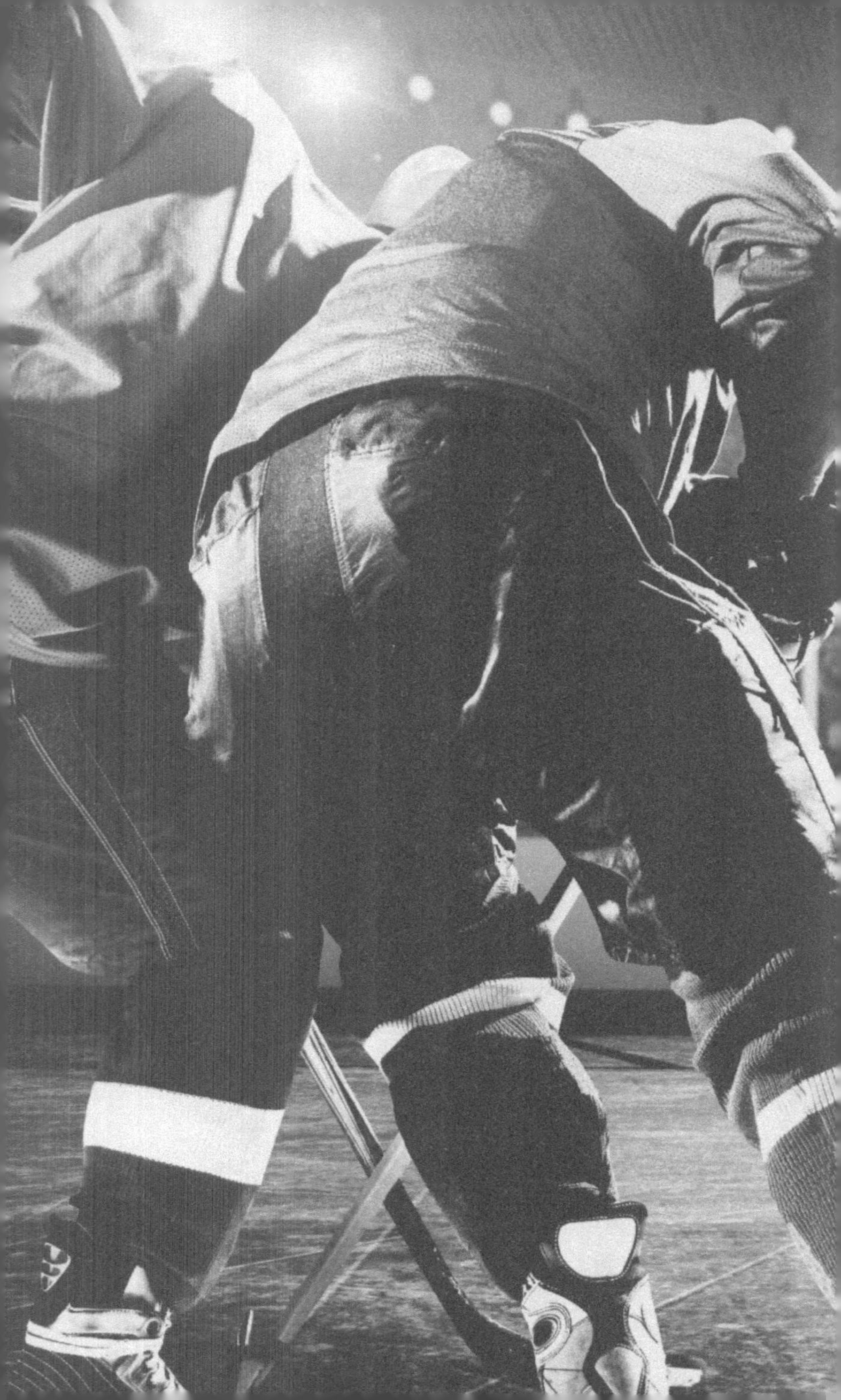

Chapter Seventeen

GRAHAM

"What's got you looking so cocky over here?" I skate over to where Noah is standing on the ice during a break in play. "We're tied."

He shrugs a shoulder. "It's only one goal to pull ahead. I feel good about tonight."

"Oh yeah?"

"Getting home. Getting you into bed."

"Fuck, Noah." Looking around, I check to be sure there is no one around us to hear his comment. "You can't say things like that right now."

"You asked."

The smile on his face is playful. It's one that I've gotten used to. I love seeing it there. Knowing that I played a part of it *being* there.

"Remind me not to be near you during the game."

"Kinda hard when we play on the same team."

Noah goes to take his spot for the face-off, leaving me shaking my head. Noah does the exact same thing to the Buffalo center as he steals the puck and takes off down the ice. The ease with which he is skating shows off his skill.

He sends the puck sailing to Marcus, deking out the defense, before he shoots it back to Noah who puts it into past the goalie.

"Fuck yeah!"

Charging down the ice, I jump onto the pile of guys surrounding Noah.

"That was a thing of beauty!"

Clapping Noah on the helmet, I love how his eyes are lit up with excitement. With less than thirty seconds left in the game, we need to step up and protect our net.

There's no way we're leaving Buffalo without the win.

And by the time the final horn sounds, the Knights have won, 4-3.

The mood in the locker room is jubilant. We're closing in on the halfway point of the season, with the All-Star break in a few weeks, and we've already won the same amount of games as we did all of last year.

It feels fucking amazing.

By the time we leave the arena, snow has been falling throughout the evening, and the wind is blowing hard as we shuffle through toward the bus.

Noah and I take our seats next to each other as Marcus and Jasper sit down across from us. Coach Andrews is on the phone when he gets on. A pinched look is on his face.

"Alright, boys. With the weather in Buffalo tonight only getting worse, we're not going anywhere."

"Shit," Marcus mutters next to me.

"We'll be here tonight and hopefully be cleared to fly out tomorrow morning."

"Not the end of the world," Noah whispers out of the corner of his mouth.

It has a shudder racking my body. Without a late flight home to Nashville, it gives us more time here together.

I don't mind the detour. It means I get to Noah faster.

"It's a good thing you scored that game-winning goal."

Noah waggles his eyebrows from his seat next to me. "What is that going to get me?"

I look around to make sure no one is watching us. Everyone is ignoring us as plans are being made. Bode is yelling about going out and getting laid.

"Maybe a blow job? My ass?"

"In that order?"

The thought of spending the night with Noah has my dick stirring in my pants. I can't seem to get enough of him.

Noah's strong hand squeezes my hand before pulling back. "I think we have all night, so why limit ourselves?"

The bus starts up, making a slow drive through the snowy streets. I'm antsy to get back to the hotel. A buzzing is taking over my body at the thought of what awaits me in our room.

I can't look at Noah for the long drive back to our hotel because it'll only have my cock grow harder. That's the last thing I need when walking off the bus.

By the time we arrive at our destination for the night, snow is blowing across the drive so we can hardly see.

Room assignments are given out as Noah takes the key to our room. There's a pep in his step as we head toward the elevator.

That fucker. Teasing me all he can as we wait for the elevator.

Bode and Dax step onto the awaiting car as we all take it up to our floors.

"You two want to go out with us?"

"Us?" Dax asks. "Speak for yourself. I'm not going out in this weather."

"Okay, Grandpa." Bode punches his bicep. "You two down?"

"Nah. I think we're going to stay in. Maybe play some video games."

Bode snorts. "Have fun."

The door opens to our floor and we get out. I follow Noah to our room, and the second we're inside, I'm on him.

"Do you think teasing me like that is fun?" I press my lips to the back of his neck. "Do you know what that does to me?"

I thrust my hips into his ass, letting him feel just how hard I am. Noah spins in my arms and throws me back against the door.

"I have a lot of fun doing it."

Noah nips at my bottom lip before thrusting his leg between mine. I'm shameless as I grind down on him. I need relief and I'll get it however he'll give it to me.

His strong hand grips my chin, turning my focus to him. As if it would be anywhere else. Noah's thumb traces my bottom lip as I watch his eyes track the movement. I dart my tongue out to lick his thumb, watching as his eyes grow hazy with lust.

I love that I can drive him as crazy as he drives me.

"Are you going to—"

I don't finish my sentence as Noah starts attacking my mouth with his. This kiss is hungry and needy. He wastes no time thrusting his tongue into my mouth.

Grabbing his jacket, I pull him closer. His cock is hard as I grind farther down onto his leg, feeling his length.

I can't wait to feel that buried inside of me. I slide one hand lower, cupping his erection as his lips trail a path down my stubbled jaw to my ear.

My groan is loud as he steps back.

"Seriously?" I whine.

I don't care if it makes me sound desperate.

I'm desperate for Noah and I'm okay if he knows it.

Noah nibbles on the throbbing pulse point in my neck. "We have all night. I want to take my time with you."

"Well, I fucking need more."

Noah pulls back, a sly grin on his face. I want to kiss it right off.

The fucker.

"Get on the bed."

I steal one last kiss before following his instructions. As I'm unbuttoning my pants, a knock echoes around the quiet hotel room.

"Open up, assholes. We've got beer."

"You've got to be kidding me," I mutter, throwing myself face-first onto the bed.

"I hate them," Noah growls. "Do you think we can ignore it and pretend we're not here?"

"Don't even think about ignoring us!" Bode's voice comes through the door. "We can't go out, so we're crashing your party."

"If I go to jail for killing them, will you come for conjugal visits?" Noah asks.

I sit up, pulling my tie over my head. "Maybe."

"Maybe?" Noah looks affronted. "Seriously?"

"You wouldn't look good in orange. Besides, we still have to win a cup together."

"Let it be known I hate this." Noah points at me before adjusting himself. "And them. I really hate them."

"Are you going to take it out on my ass later?"

If looks could kill…

"I hate you more now."

I wink at him, adjusting my fast-deflating dick. "A little taste of your own medicine."

"I guess if I kill you too, I don't have to worry about conjugal visits."

"Open up!" The bang comes louder this time.

"Chill out," Noah shouts at them before swinging open the door. "I thought you were going out?"

Bode shakes his head as he walks into the room. A brown paper bag is dropped by my feet on the bed. "Can't. No cars to go out, but at least there's a convenience store next door."

"I kept trying to tell him it's not safe," Dax tells us.

"I listened, didn't I?" Bode grabs a six-pack of beer from the bag and hands one to each of us. "Couldn't get Jasper and Marcus out of their rooms."

"Weren't you guys hanging out?" Dax points at the blank TV. "I thought you were playing video games?"

Noah brushes by him, cracking open his drink and flopping back onto his bed. "We just hadn't started yet."

"Awesome. C'mon, Dax."

The two of them fire up the TV and the game system that we travel with. Seeing how it's small enough to connect to the TV, it makes it easy to bring to play during downtime.

My phone buzzes in my pocket.

NOAH

Still considering murder

GRAHAM

No you're not

No, but now I've got a wicked case of blue balls and can't do anything about it

Think we could kick them out early? You're not the only one with that issue

You deserve it after your teasing

So you're not going to help me with it then?
Don't want to give me a blow job?

Stop. It.

Payback is a bitch

See if I fuck you tonight

No one is getting any as long as they're in
our room

"WHAT HAS YOU SMILING SO HARD?" Dax asks, turning his attention away from the video game toward me.

"What? Nothing."

I fumble to lock my phone and throw it face down on the bed. The last thing I want is to have the guys see who I'm texting. Better yet, what I'm texting about.

"Nothing? That was not the face of nothing," Bode points out. He sips his beer, checking his own phone.

"You seeing someone?" Dax asks.

"No one special." I brush it off, sipping on my drink.

The words taste like lead coming out of my mouth. I sneak a glance over at Noah, and he's shoving his phone into his pocket, not looking at me. There's a hard look on his face that even I can see from here.

The set of his jaw tells me he doesn't like what I said.

But is there any way to make it better? To backtrack and not say those words?

Fuck.

A heaviness settles over me as the guys keep playing video games and shooting the shit around us. It's hard to pay attention when I feel like I made things weird between Noah and me.

It's not like I can have this conversation with him in front of the guys. I can't text him because what would I say? Sorry, I didn't mean it?

It's not like Noah isn't special, but wasn't this whole thing supposed to be temporary? To see if whatever I'm feeling is for him, or if it might be for others?

Right now, all I want is Noah. But I'm not sure how to cross that bridge of wanting to make this thing with him more permanent.

If only we didn't get stuck in Buffalo. Then I wouldn't be screwing things up and worrying about what this thing with Noah is.

FUCK. Something feels good. A wet heat enveloping my cock. That mouth is talented as they slide up and down my dick. I thrust upward, moaning as a strong hand starts to play with my balls.

"Mmm."

A warm breath over my slit has me peeking my eyes open.

"About damn time."

Noah is lying between my thighs with a devious smile on his face. His thumb drags through the slit before he swallows me down to the base.

"Fuuuuck."

I don't know if I've ever had a better blow job than by his mouth. Fisting my hand in Noah's hair, I thrust up into his mouth. The sound of him sucking has my balls drawing up tight and ready to empty into his mouth.

"Noah. Fuck—" Before I can come, Noah pops off me, wiping his mouth. "What the fuck?"

He's sitting on his knees on the bed before me, his cock sticking straight out from him. His hard muscles are on display for me. If I had more patience, I'd spend the morning licking and kissing every ab of his.

"You're not coming until my dick is buried inside you."

"Then do it."

Noah hops off the bed, and I pop up onto my elbow to admire the view.

The strong muscles in his back.

His ass that you could bounce a quarter off.

The light dusting of hair on his thick thighs.

Fuck.

Noah Fields is the sexiest person in the world, and it should scare me how quickly I'm becoming addicted to the man.

I don't want anyone else but him.

"Want to help?" Noah tosses the travel lube and it lands next to me on the bed.

Opening the packet, I pour more than is needed onto my fingers to start working myself open. Watching as Noah gives himself a slow stroke has me shoving three fingers in my ass. It burns, but I want Noah.

I didn't get him last night because the guys interrupted our night. Now, I want him more than anything.

"I'm ready."

"You sure?"

I nod. I don't want to waste another minute.

Noah lies next to me and pushes my leg up. His hard chest lines up with my back as he notches the head of his dick against my hole. Strong hands roam the planes of my stomach as he starts to push inside.

"Yessss," I hiss out.

"Fuck. You feel amazing."

Noah doesn't stop until he's balls deep inside of me. Reaching behind, I grasp his thigh and hold him into me.

"Fuck me, Noah."

Noah takes my words to heart and pulls out before slamming back inside me. Warm lips press kisses into my back as his hand jacks me off.

Each thrust against my prostate has me ready to explode. Every nerve is firing on all synapses. My skin is buzzing.

This time with Noah feels different from any time before it.

"I want you to come for me, Graham. I want you to come all over this bed because it's my cock in your ass."

"Yes. I'm almost there."

"You love my dick, don't you?"

"You know I do."

Turning my head, I find Noah's lips in a savage kiss. It's rough and hard as he continues pegging my ass. Closing my hand over his, I squeeze harder.

It takes a few more thrusts before I'm erupting over our hands. Ropes of cum spill out as I feel Noah unload his own release inside me.

"Fuck, Graham."

"I know."

Grabbing his hand off me, I keep him close. I'm not ready to let Noah go. I don't know if I'll ever be able to let him go.

Being with Noah, just the two of us, pushes every thought out of my head. This is all that matters. The two of us connecting.

The rest will come however it comes.

And I'll worry about it when it does.

Chapter Eighteen

GRAHAM

"You're calling that a penalty?" Coach Andrews yells at the ref. "If that's high sticking, I don't know what a high stick actually is!"

Boos are raining down on us as Coach is yelling at the refs. Bode is being escorted into the sin bin. His anger can be felt from here.

Since the start of the game with Boston, it's been nothing but a fight. We're skating hard. Have good control of the puck. But no matter what we seem to be doing, they're ahead of us. They have a split second on us from where we'll be and are recovering the puck from our zone that much faster.

It shows in the score too. They're up 3-0.

It fucking sucks.

"Fisher. You're up. Don't let them score on another power play."

Hopping over the bench, I head onto the ice as the puck is dropped to start play again. Noah is there, grabbing the puck from Jasper, but before he can do anything with it, he's slammed into the boards and Boston takes over.

Fuck.

We've been on the defensive the entire game and can't seem to make our own attack. Skating hard, I slide my stick out to intercept the puck, but again, he's already gone.

"Damn it!"

Dax is there, but another Boston player is blocking him before they send the puck flying into the back of our net.

The crowd erupts around us as Bode leaves the penalty box. He's pounding his fist into his helmet, visibly upset.

With the score now 4-0 late in the second period, we're going to have to fight to get any kind of ground in this game.

Morale is low in the locker room, no matter how much Coach and Marcus try to pep us up during the intermission.

An early goal from Marcus in the third period closes the gap, but when they answer a few minutes later with a goal of their own, our collective bubble pops.

After that, we can't seem to do anything right. It's like the entire team forgot how to play.

And we end up having our worst loss of the season, 6-2.

Fuck.

"This sucks," Noah tells me as the two of us head off the ice.

"I can't tell you the last time a loss felt this terrible."

Back in the early days when I started playing for the Knights, it seemed like all we could do was lose in spectacular fashion. Now that we've all had a taste of how good winning feels, of seeing where we can go, it's hard.

Each loss feels worse when we know what we're

capable of. Sure, Boston is a good team, but they aren't the best team in the league right now.

Which makes this loss a tougher pill to swallow.

"I thought we had a chance when Marcus scored," Jasper tells us as we drop down onto our seats in the visitors' locker room.

The cold, dark gray of the room doesn't do much to improve the low morale. Everyone is feeling this loss keenly.

"Tonight was a tough one, men," Coach Andrews tells us. "I'm not going to lie, I thought we could turn things around in the third period. But we can't win them all, no matter how much we want to."

"It's going to be a long ride home," Dax groans from next to me.

"I know it will," Coach answers. "But we're going to take tonight. And then tomorrow, once we're home, we're going to study the film, find the mistakes, and then work on cleaning them up. Learn from this game to make sure we don't have a repeat performance."

His gaze looks around the entire locker room, studying each man in here. "This team has grit. We have determination. I know what everyone said when they fired Boyd halfway through the season and brought me in. It sucks. But I know we can be the kind of team people fear playing because they know we're that good. We have potential. Don't let this loss convince you otherwise."

This is why I love playing for Coach Andrews. He's worlds better than our old coach. Boyd didn't seem to have the charisma that Andrews has to lead a team.

Even though we lost, he makes it seem like it isn't the end of the world. When it really isn't. It's just a game.

Stripping out of my gear, I hit the showers and change

into my suit to leave the arena. A few of the guys are talking to the press. Thank God I don't have to.

Even though I played well, I don't feel like I'd have much to comment about it tonight.

"You ready?"

Noah grabs his bag and slings it over his shoulder as I stand, grabbing mine too.

"Ready to get home."

"It feels like we've been gone for months," Noah tells me.

"Feels like it," Marcus agrees as he walks out with us. "I hate the long road stretches."

"I just want to sleep in my own bed," I whine. "I hate road hotel rooms."

"Do you think Boston knows where we stay and changes out the mattresses to make them the worst in the entire world?" Dax jogs up to us as the cold night air greets us as we head outside.

"Wouldn't put it past 'em." Noah nods in thanks to the security guy as fans are lining up around the barricades.

A few Nashville fans are in attendance as guys sign autographs for them. The downside? Drunk Boston fans are also lining up to sling insults our way.

"Too bad you couldn't pull off the win. The Knights suck!" someone throws out. "Bet you wish you were still playing for Colorado, Fields!"

"What a dick," I mutter under my breath as I give a Sharpie back to someone after signing their jersey.

"Just ignore them," Noah whispers to me.

"Aww. Crying to your boyfriend? I don't think he can make this feel better for you."

"Nice one, bro."

I stop dead in my tracks and turn toward the voices.

The men, looking to be in their late fifties based on their appearance, are high-fiving one another.

"Keep walking. They're just being dickheads."

Jasper pushes me forward, but the gut feeling that sinks in my stomach is a hard one to swallow.

I move toward the bus in a fog. Listening to their words on repeat.

Crying to your boyfriend?

Honestly? I have no idea what Noah and I are to each other. It feels like more than just a friends-with-benefits situation. If this thing were to end tomorrow, I don't know if I'd want to be with anyone but Noah.

But does that mean I'm ready to be out to the world? Based on that guy's comments, I don't know if I could take it. One well-timed insult has my head spinning.

"You know they didn't mean anything by that, right?" Noah tells me as he takes his seat next to me on the bus.

"Right."

They might not have meant anything by it, but it feels like something to me. I'm sure Noah has heard it all before. It doesn't make it okay.

Noah pats my leg as the bus pulls out of the arena and heads toward the airport. Pulling out my headphones, I pop them into my ears and crank a noisy playlist.

I need to get lost in something other than my thoughts. I'm not quite sure how to handle what that guy said.

If Noah and I were together for real, the comments would be even worse than that. Is that something I'm ready for? Is that something I can handle?

I don't know if I'm at that point yet. Does that mean this thing with Noah has to end? I'm not sure if I'm ready for that either.

Fuck me. I have no idea what I'm ready for, and it's all because of one drunk-ass fan.

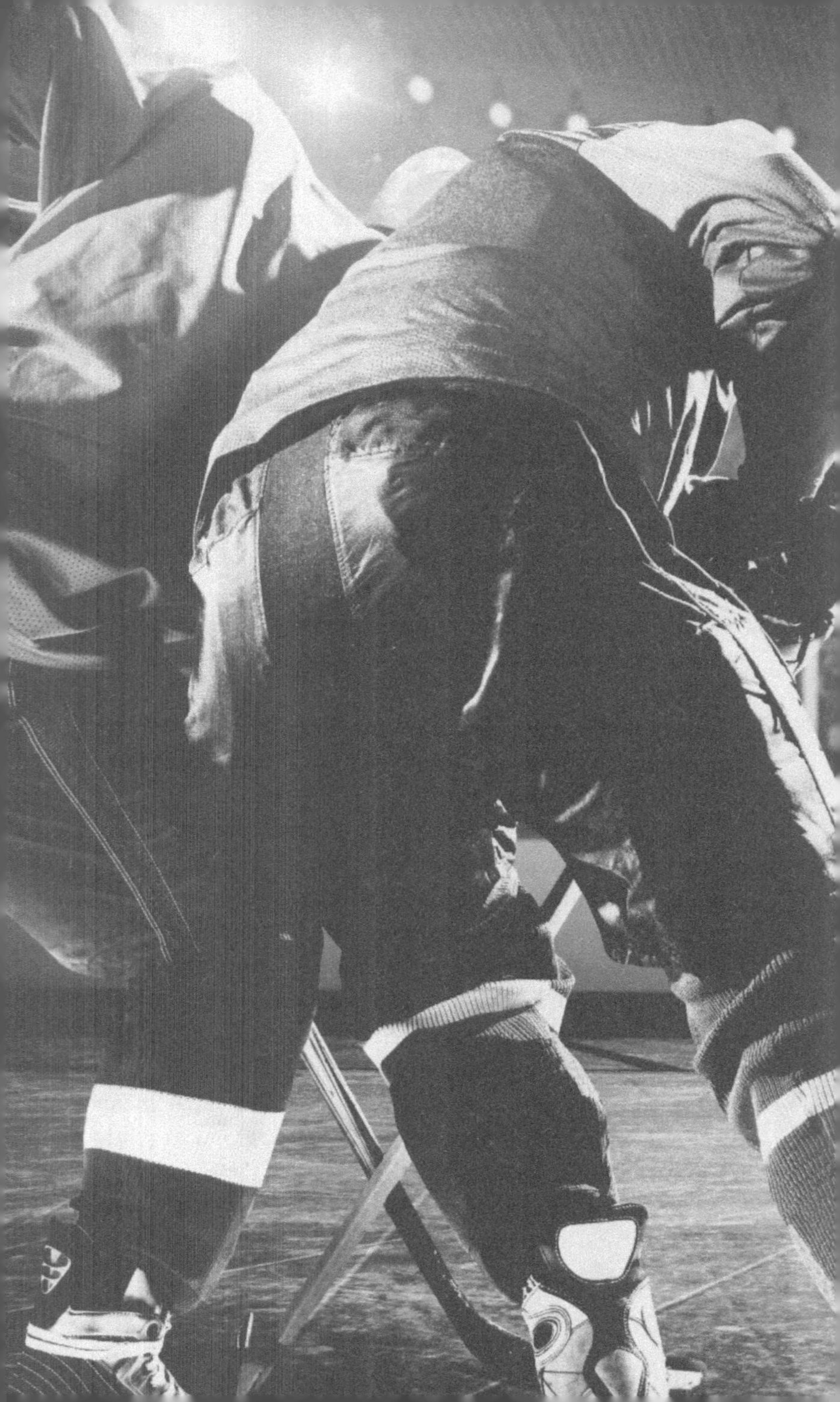

Chapter Nineteen

NOAH

I t's late in the afternoon when I wake up. With the
season more than half over and a late game tonight, I
needed the extra sleep. The clouds hang heavy outside my
window.

Considering that I spend most of my time at the rink
or in Graham's room, the decorations in here are pretty
pitiful. As in, I put nothing up.

Grabbing a T-shirt to throw on, I head out into the
living room to find Graham, but it's dark with no one in
sight.

My phone sits on the charger in the kitchen. Walking
over, I fire off a text.

NOAH

Where are you?

GRAHAM

At the store

Why?

> Just woke up. Didn't realize you left

And disrupt your pregame nap? I know
better than that 🌚

A SMILE SLIDES across my face at the words that pop up on my screen. It's one of the many things that Graham and I have come to learn about each other over the last few months. Even through text, I can feel his playfulness. It's something that's been missing since that dickhead made those comments when we were in Boston last week.

I could see how much they affected him even when he tried to hide it. It's something I've had years of practice to be able to brush off.

NOAH

> Maybe you can interrupt my post-
> game nap?

GRAHAM

Is it a nap if you're going to bed?

> Hopefully going to bed with you...

Oh yeah?

ANOTHER TEXT POPS up on my phone, this one also making me smile because of who it's from. But the name of the group has me snort laughing.

<<BLACK DIAMONDS BADASSES>>
NICK

Think you guys can beat Detroit tonight?

NOAH

Yes.

Who let Cash rename the chat?

CASH

It should have been renamed a long
time ago

TROY

I said no

CASH

And I ignored you

NICK

And I didn't get in the middle of it

I LAUGH, because this is exactly like them. It's one of the things I missed most when I left Denver. These guys are my family. I didn't want to trade them for anything. But before I knew it, I had my own family here in Nashville.

NOAH

I'm surprised you haven't kicked me out yet

TROY

Nah. Once a Black Diamond, always a
Black Diamond

Even though I'm a Knight now?

Cash

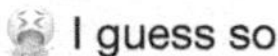 I guess so

Fuck off

We're going to kick your ass again in a few weeks

CASH

Pretty cocky there

Not if we can back it up

TROY

Keep up the trash talk. It's going to make beating you even sweeter

CASH

Besides, would you really want to beat your best friends and hurt their feelings?

GRAHAM INTERRUPTS my texts with the guys. The person that I want to be talking to. More than these guys.

GRAHAM

What did you have in mind?

NICK

You wouldn't want to do that

CASH

He loves us too much to hurt our feelings

NOAH

First I'm going to get you in the shower and
then get you in bed

NICK

Umm....

TROY

Have we entered an alternative world?
What is going on?

OH FUCK. Oh fuck, oh fuck.

Oh. Fuck.

I didn't even realize how quickly that text popped up,
and I tapped on it by accident.

CASH

Wait, are you seeing someone?

NOAH

No

TROY

Then why do you want to get someone
into bed?

CASH

Piper hasn't told me anything

Because I haven't told Piper

CASH

So you are seeing someone

NICK

I haven't heard anything either

TROY

Me either. I thought we were friends, Noah.

It's like he leaves the city and forgets all
about us

NICK

Or forgets that he can, you know, text us

You guys are too busy

NICK

Never too busy for you

CASH

We always have time for you, Strawberry

Ugh. I was hoping to drop that nickname
when I left

TROY

Never

CASH

You're just making it worse for yourself by
denying it

I'm hanging up now

NICK

You can't actually hang up a text

You know what I mean

CASH

Such a baby

Gotta get my head right for the game

GRAHAM

Where'd you go?

Did you check out on me?

NOAH

Fuck off losers

GRAHAM

Did I miss something?

SERIOUSLY. Fuck me. Can I not keep my texts straight? It's not like it's hard.

NOAH

Sorry. That wasn't meant for you

NICK

What wasn't meant for us?

Okay. The equivalent of hanging up a call is what I'm doing to you fuckers.

CASH

Aww. He needs to go text his boyfriend

No I don't

TROY

He totally is.

CASH

I can't wait to tell Piper

Tell Piper and I'll kill you

CASH

You'd never do it. You'd miss your future
brother-in-law too much

No, I don't think I will

I LOCK my phone screen to prevent any other misfired text messages. If it's in my pocket, maybe I won't accidentally make an idiot of myself. Or worse, out Graham.

Fuck. That'd be the worst thing in the world.

"Hey." Graham is walking through the front door, grocery bag in hand, startling me.

"Hi."

"You okay?" He eyes me as he sets the bag down on the counter.

"Sorry. I was texting with the guys and couldn't seem to text the right person."

"You didn't—"

"I didn't send them anything I shouldn't have. Might have hinted I'm seeing someone, but not much more than that."

I don't miss the relief that my words give him. I hate it. I hate that we're not on the same page about what we're doing here.

"I didn't think you would. But good to check."

"Right."

Graham puts the groceries away before heading toward his room. I watch the tension in his shoulders release as he walks away from me.

Maybe this means time has run out on the two of us. That we should both move on. If we call it quits now, maybe it'll be easier than if we keep it going.

As much as I want to continue being with him, I think

it's run its course. That conversation is something that I have time to figure out.

Because it's not a right-now conversation.

That's for later.

Right now, the only thing I need to be focusing on is Detroit. Getting the win for the Knights.

After?

After, I can figure out what this thing with Graham has become.

It's no longer a friends-with-benefits situation. Or a roommates-with-benefits situation. I don't know what it is to him, but it's a hell of a lot more to me.

We can't call it a relationship. Hell, would I even know what one looks like since I've never been in a serious one? What Graham and I have has been the most real thing in my life.

How can a few short texts put me so on edge? It tells me we are not anywhere close to being on the same page.

Fuck. I hate when feelings get involved.

Because now I have no idea what I'm going to do.

Chapter Twenty

NOAH

"I know you guys know what everyone is saying. I don't need to repeat it to you."

Coach is standing in front of all of us, excited energy radiating off him. The Knights are in a position no one thought we would be in at this point in the year.

With a few more wins, we could be looking at the play-offs, something that hasn't happened in years. It's so close, we can taste it. Everyone wants it.

But no one is saying it. We don't want to jinx ourselves.

"The home crowd is going to be rocking tonight, so let's go out there and play how I know we can play and bring home the W!"

"Alright, men." Marcus calls all of us to the center of the locker room. "You heard Coach. We've played under pressure before, so let's not let this get to us. Go out there and play Knights Hockey. Knights on three. One, two, three…"

"Knights!"

"Think we got this?" Graham asks as we head down the tunnel.

The noise of the crowd is loud and echoing around us.

"You know it." I elbow him in the side as we hit the ice to music and lights flashing around the arena. Every fan is decked out in red for the game tonight.

This has always been one of my favorite parts of the game—the energy before it starts. It's a living, breathing thing. A live wire of excitement.

I feed off it.

When the game gets tough, this is what I think about. About the fans.

A few Detroit faithful stand out in their black jerseys, but it's almost all Nashville fans tonight.

"Detroit is a good team."

"We're better." Graham shoots me a subtle wink as we skate to the bench.

The game starts and we easily take control. The way we're moving as a team and anticipating each other's moves is incredible. It feels easy.

Easier still when Marcus puts the biscuit in the basket in the middle of the first period. We keep that same energy during the first intermission and carry it into the second period.

Detroit doesn't lie down. They're battling it out and end up getting one past our goalie.

As soon as play starts again, I'm fighting for the puck. There's no way I'm going to let this guy beat me. Until I'm flying through the air as my skates come out from under me. My momentum propels me forward too fast as I hit the pipes and go crashing into the boards.

That's it.

Lights out.

GRAHAM

I'M GOING to be sick.

Noah crumpling to the ice like that wasn't natural. The angle at which he hit and flew into the boards is something I haven't seen in all my years of playing hockey.

The guy who took him out is kneeling next to him, shaking him. I vaguely register the whistles around me as the refs skate over to him and push the opposing player off him. Medical personnel are already coming onto the ice to check on Noah.

And I'm glued to my spot on the ice.

Noah went down.

Even in all the hits he's taken, he's bounced up. Or at least showed signs of pain.

Now? He's not moving. No rolling on the ice or clutching at his arm to indicate he's okay, just hurt. Noah is curled up on the ice with his arm under him at an awkward angle.

Dropping down to one knee, I bury my head in my gloved fist. The anxiety burning through me is threatening to overwhelm me.

Noah has to be okay. There's no way he can't be.

"He's going to be okay," Marcus tells me. His words are fuzzy. There's a buzzing in my brain as I watch Noah being loaded onto a stretcher.

"Is he?" I whisper.

The crowd is cheering for him as he's taken off the ice. My guess? Headed straight to a local hospital. I can't imagine what his parents must be feeling after watching him take that hit.

"Bring it in, guys!" Coach yells from the bench.

"Take a few minutes. Get your heads on straight and

then we'll restart the game," one of the refs tells the coach as I skate to where the team is all huddled together.

"Look," Coach Andrews starts, "watching that was hard. But Noah wouldn't want us to get lost in our heads. I want us to band together, play hard, and win this game for Noah, okay?"

There's muffled words from the team. I don't know if anyone is going to be able to get their head in the game long enough to play the way we want to.

There's still a period and a half left to play.

As the guys start to break apart and hit the ice, Coach calls me to him. "You going to be okay, Graham?"

"I…I'm worried about him."

"I know. We all are. I promise, you can head to the hospital after the game and see him, okay?"

"Sure."

I swallow around the bile building in my throat. Seeing Noah in the hospital might break me. Seeing him unconscious, maybe worse? I don't know if I can handle it.

I don't know if *my heart* can handle it.

"If you can't go, tell me now. I can sit you right now."

Taking a deep breath, I take the water bottle one of the trainers hands me.

I take a swig and clear my head. "No, Coach. I got this."

Coach studies me, and whatever he sees on my face convinces him that I can do this. Because like he said, Noah wouldn't want us to cave.

The only thing that keeps me going is the home crowd. They don't sit down for the rest of the game. Their cheers give me the boost I need to push everything from my brain.

Hockey. Keeping the puck out of our zone so our team

can put points on the scoreboard. That's it. That's the only thing that matters.

Nothing else.

And when the final horn sounds, what feels like hours later, the Knights come out on top.

Finally. Finally.

I somehow make it through the post-game interview. Every journalist asks about Noah and how it affected our play. I want to smack them. What do they think?

I don't know what the film will show, but I don't care.

All that matters is getting to Noah right now.

Chapter Twenty-One

GRAHAM

"Are you going to go see Noah?" Jasper asks as we make our way out of the arena.

"Yeah."

"Do you think they'll let you see him?" Dax asks from next to me.

I shrug. "I don't know. But hopefully I can."

"If you can, tell him we're all pulling for him, yeah?" Jasper tells me as he claps me on the back.

"Sure thing." I nod at him before heading to Noah's truck.

Considering that we rode here together, it's the only means I have of getting home. I hated fishing through his locker to grab his keys.

But here we are.

The entire drive to the hospital, dread clings to me. I haven't been able to turn off the moment Noah went down on the ice. It keeps replaying in my head.

The way he dropped.

The way he didn't move.

The way he was carted off the ice.

I wouldn't wish it on my worst enemy.

And for it to happen to Noah?

I have to pull the truck over to take a minute to breathe. To let the moment of wanting to get sick pass.

Fuck.

You can do this, Graham. Suck it up and go check on Noah. He would do the same for you if the roles were reversed and you were in the hospital.

Another deep breath.

Okay. I got this.

My phone buzzes in my pocket. Pulling it out, my parents' names light up the screen.

MOM

Tenley called. They're on their way to Nashville, but put you on the approved visitors list for Noah. He's in the ICU

DAD

Let us know how he's doing.

GRAHAM

Okay

ICU? God. That can't be good.

DAD

How are you holding up?

MOM

It's always hard to see a teammate and friend go down like that

GRAHAM

I'm okay. Promise.

MOM

Love you, Graham

Love you too, Mom

LOCKING MY PHONE, I shove it into my pocket. That sick feeling is back.

It's a lie. A bald-faced lie because Mom's words have a lead weight dropping into my stomach.

A teammate and friend?

If Noah was simply a teammate and friend, I don't think I'd be feeling what I'm feeling right now. Putting the truck back into drive, I head toward the hospital.

No sense in delaying this any longer. It won't get easier the longer I wait.

The rest of the drive goes by in a blur. I have no idea what is waiting for me on the other side of the hospital door.

The thick smell of disinfectant hangs heavy in the halls. I follow the signs toward the ICU where a nurse is waiting at the desk just beyond the elevator doors.

"Hi. I'm here to see Noah Fields."

"Are you on the approved visitors list?"

"Yes. Graham Fisher."

She taps away on her keyboard as I take in the wide-open space. Glass doors are pulled tight with curtains to hide the patients from prying eyes. Machines are beeping as nurses flit between the rooms.

"The doctor is in with him now, but if you take a seat, we'll let you see him once they're gone."

"Okay. Thank you."

The nurse points to a bank of seats behind me and I sink into one of them.

More waiting.

More worrying.

More time to think.

Every time I shift, the hard plastic of the seat beneath me groans. With every blink, I'm back out there on that ice, seeing him go down.

Is Noah going to be okay?

I've seen some pretty hard hits playing hockey, but that one? It has panic taking hold inside me and not letting go.

"Mr. Fisher?"

I glance up, seeing the nurse, a bulky man who could dwarf me, stopping in front of me.

"That's me."

"You can see Mr. Fields now. He's not awake, but if you're quiet, you can stay in there with him for a few minutes."

"Okay. How's he doing?"

"He took a pretty bad hit to his shoulder and has a concussion. We're going to keep a close eye on him, but he's stable." I follow him down the hallway where he points to a door on the left. "In there."

"Thanks."

The lights are dim when I enter and pull the curtain back. The muted light above his bed casts Noah in a soft glow.

It has my stomach sinking further seeing him laid up like this. His arm is in a sling, stabilized on his chest, with a cut across the bridge of his nose with a butterfly bandage covering it.

The normally larger-than-life Noah looks small.

"Fuck," I mutter.

Grabbing the chair next to the bed, I drop down into it. It's a bit more comfortable than the plastic chairs in the waiting room, but I'm painfully aware that it's too small for my frame.

Time seems to move too fast, but not fast enough. The beeping of the machine is the only sound echoing around the room. A nurse comes in to check on him, but leaves almost immediately, seemingly happy with everything.

I'm not. I want to shout after her to come back so I can ask how he's doing. Get a better update than the one I got when I first came in.

Noah stirs.

"Noah?" I drop my hand on the edge of the bed. "Can you hear me?"

I stand and move closer as he lets out a soft moan.

"Graham?" his voice croaks out.

"I'm here, Noah. I'm here. It's okay."

I want to reach out and touch him, but I don't know where. I don't want to cause him any more pain than he's already in.

Scared brown eyes squint against the light as they search the room for the sound of my voice.

"Don't try to move."

Noah reaches out a hand, the one closest to me that's not in a sling, but before I can take it, a nurse comes strutting in. I fly back, knocking the chair I was sitting in over.

"Fuck," I mutter, setting it upright.

"The patient needs quiet," the older nurse chides me.

"Sorry," I whisper back.

Glancing over at Noah, his eyes are shut again. A pained look rests on his face.

Fuck. *Fuck.*

The last thing I want to do is anything to cause Noah

any kind of physical pain, but based on the reaction I just had, I might have caused him a different kind of pain.

"Mr. Fields needs quiet and rest. You can come back and see him tomorrow during visiting hours."

"Okay." I look at the nurse, voicing my question to her. "He'll be okay, right?"

This time, when she looks at me, her face is softer. "You never know with concussions and the brain, but he's been waking up off and on. That's a good sign."

"Okay. Thank you."

I nod at the nurse before taking one last look at Noah. He's out again.

My heart is in my throat as I leave. I have no idea what is going to happen.

But I have a feeling that everything just changed.

For both of us.

Chapter Twenty-Two

NOAH

"Is there anything you need?" Mom asks, not for the first time this week.

"I'm okay."

I lean back, trying to adjust my pillow, but moving my arm makes my entire body ache. I try to hide the pain, but Mom is better than that. It's like she has an eagle eye for any kind of physical pain her children might be in.

"You're not. Do you need more pain meds?"

The last thing I want is to be in a drug-induced stupor. I was in and out of it all last week, and I don't want to feel like that again. Even though my shoulder and head are down to a dull throb, I'd rather suck it up and deal with it than be on more meds.

"I don't want them, Mom."

"Should we check with the doctor?"

Mom is pressing the buzzer on the side of my bed before I even have a chance to tell her no. Dad is still sitting in the corner, trying not to laugh.

It's not like I can blame her for fussing. I've only been given a brief recap of what happened out there on the ice and that's it. From the sound of it, I don't want to see the footage of me going down.

The nurse, Kyla, strides into the room with purpose. She's been one of my main nurses during the day, and has kept me sane. Hopefully I'll only be here a few more days.

"Everything okay in here?" she asks, checking my stats.

"I'm fine."

"He's in pain."

My mom and I answer at the same time.

"Do you want anything, Noah?" Kyla asks.

"I don't." I adjust ever so slightly to face my mom. Her face has been showing nothing but worry for the last however many days I've been in the hospital. Trying to count the days is too much. "Mom, do you think you could maybe go to the cafeteria and get me something to eat?"

"Is that okay?" she asks Kyla.

"That's more than fine." Kyla shoots a wink in my direction.

"Okay. I'll be back." Mom drops a kiss on my cheek before leaving the room.

"Just buzz if you need anything."

"Thanks, Kyla."

"And for what it's worth, the team is going to miss you."

"Wait, what?" I do a double take at her words, a fierce slice of pain cutting through my head.

She looks chagrined. "You haven't heard?"

"Heard what?" I look to Dad, and he's scrubbing a hand over his stubbled jaw. "What aren't you telling me?"

"Crap," Kyla mutters. "I thought someone would have told you by now."

"Told me what?"

"The team put you on IR," Dad tells me, walking over to my side of the bed.

"Fuck." I close my eyes, thinking of the implications of this.

I hear the door click shut and peek one eye open. It's just me and my dad in here now. I hate that I'm in the hospital. For the second time in three years, my playing time has been cut short.

Am I jinxed? Am I not meant to play? Why the hell does this keep happening to me?"

"Look at me, Noah." Dad's voice is hard, telling me I better listen. Even though I'm over thirty, if I don't listen, I still feel like I could get grounded.

Is that a feeling that ever goes away?

"It's not the end of the world. I promise you that."

"Why does it feel like it is?" My voice shakes.

"It happened to me. Trust me, it wasn't."

"But this is the second time this has happened to me. What if—"

"Hey." Dad clasps my forearm that's resting on the bed. "You can't play the what-if game. It's not going to get you anywhere."

I want to bang my head against the pillows, but I can't. It seems like I can't do much of anything these days except lie in a hospital bed.

And I fucking hate it.

"What good am I to the team if I'm on IR? My knee injury and now this? It fucking sucks, Dad. All I want to do is play and I can't do that. So sorry if I can't see the bright side right now."

Dad smirks. "It's a good thing your mom isn't here to hear you say that."

"Well, it does."

"Injured reserved means the team doesn't want to risk you hurting yourself any more. They care about your future with the team and want to make sure you come back better than ever next year."

"Really?" I scoff. "And what if I can't come back next year? What if this is the injury that finally takes me out?"

The lights are starting to become too bright. This is what sucks. I'll be feeling okay for a little while, but then the headache will come back and knock me on my ass. The doctor said this could happen for at least a few weeks.

Then why am I surprised I'm on IR?

I only hope these mood swings won't last forever. I'm tired of feeling like this.

Dad nods. "I know it might not be the easiest thing to hear, but you need to take this time to heal. To get your head and your body in the right space to be able to rehab and come back next year."

"I want to tell you you're right." I sigh.

"It can be hard to admit. When all we want to do is play the game we love, it can suck to be sidelined."

Some of my earliest memories are of going to the games to watch my dad play. I wasn't around for when he was injured, but after the Mountain Lions Super Bowl when my sister was born, he retired. Said it was time. He wanted to put family first. It was around the time that I took to hockey, and he became my biggest fan. Just like I was for him out on the field. My dad could do no wrong in my eyes. Having that support system made it easy to adapt to the NHL.

But for how much longer?

"You know," Dad starts, "IR was the best thing that ever could have happened to me."

"You don't need to try and make me feel better about it."

"I'm not. If I hadn't been injured, your mom wouldn't have come to help me rehab and keep an eye on me, and I never would've realized that we were meant for each other."

"Really?"

Dad nods. "Really. Best fucking thing to ever happen to me. If it weren't for that asshole who took me out again during the game, I might never have realized how much I love your mother. You and Piper wouldn't be here, and that's not a world I want to live in. You, your mom, and your sister are everything to me."

Closing my eyes, I try to hold back the tears. I knew that my dad's injury brought them together, but hearing how much he loves her? Loves us? It's more than I can stomach right about now.

My heart is bruised and battered more than my head and shoulder. Because in my moment of need, the man I was falling for pushed me away.

I have no idea how he's feeling because I haven't seen him since that fateful night. Sure, I've gotten a few texts checking in on how I'm feeling, but that's it.

Or so I'm told. Because Mom took my phone away and won't let me have it.

Even though he pushed me away, I still want him here for the exact reasons my dad just said. I want someone to hold my hand and tell me it's all going to work out. That I'll be able to rejoin the team next season without missing a beat.

Even if it doesn't feel that way right now. Everything is too raw and uncertain. Taking a deep breath, I try to push down those feelings and give my head a break.

"I think I need sleep," I mumble, not opening my eyes.

"We'll be here when you wake up."

The warmth of my dad's hand covering mine is the balm I need to keep my frayed nerves in check. Everything about these last few days has stirred up more inside me than I ever cared to admit.

I was falling for Graham. Hell, I fell harder for him than any man I've ever met. So much for keeping it to a friends-with-benefits situation.

Muffled sounds hit my ears as the room door opens and closes.

"Is he sleeping?" Mom's voice is there, but I don't hear the answer. Only my dad's words to her.

"I love you, Tenley. More than you'll ever know."

Those are the last words I hear as sleep once again takes me under.

Chapter Twenty-Three

NOAH

"**A**re you ready to get out of here, Noah?" The door to my hospital room swings open and the doctor and his interns walk in.

"Fuck, yes."

"Noah!" Mom chides me.

The doctor laughs. "It's okay. I wouldn't want to be cooped up here any longer."

"See, Mom? Even the doctor agrees."

"Mainly because I wouldn't be able to survive on the food."

"I'm ready to get home to my place and make my own food."

"Wait." A panicked look comes over Mom's face. Something I'm very familiar with these last few weeks. Any time I shifted, she'd start hovering to make sure I was okay. "Who is going to take care of him?"

"Mom." I don't roll my eyes at her—only because I don't want to get my ass handed to me. "I'm thirty-one. I can stay on my own."

"Actually," the doctor starts, "for the next few weeks

you should have someone with you. In case you have any setbacks, you want someone to be able to take you to the hospital."

Oh, fuck me. The exact wrong words to say to my mother.

"What about Graham?" Dad asks. There's a placating tone to his voice. I know he's doing it to try and appease me, but I know Mom. Mom won't hear it.

"Graham? The same guy who hasn't been to see Noah in the hospital once? That Graham?" Okay, maybe Mom is more annoyed for reasons other than I thought. "Forget that, but he has games to play. What if he's away and Noah has an episode?"

"An episode?" I ask.

"Any sudden headaches, and we'd want to know immediately," the doctor tells us.

"Are we able to take him home with us?" Mom asks. "To Denver, I mean. We'd be able to have him with us to keep a better eye on him."

"He would be cleared to fly, so I don't see why you couldn't do that."

"That settles that." Mom sticks her hand out to shake the doctor's hand. "Thank you for everything you've done to help take care of Noah. I'll never forget it."

"We want to see our star player back on the ice next season. The nurse will be in shortly for discharge. I hope I don't see you again."

"Thanks, Doc. I can say the same to you."

After he leaves, I breathe a sigh of relief. Even though I won't be rejoining the team, at least I won't have to be staring at a hospital ceiling for the next however many days.

"Are we able to stop by my place before we head home?" I ask as soon as they're gone.

Dad nods. "We have plenty of time. The team owner said we can use their plane to get home, so I don't think they'd mind if we have a stowaway."

I laugh, and for the first time, it doesn't hurt. Maybe there is an end in sight to this whole ordeal. Even if my body is starting to heal, the process of my heart healing might not happen immediately.

Because I still haven't talked to Graham. And if I leave for Denver tonight, I don't know when I'll see him next.

I don't want to run out of town without having the chance to talk to him. What I'll say to him? I guess we'll cross that bridge when we get there.

THE DRIVE from the hospital to home seems never-ending. With each passing minute, the nerves in my stomach threaten to overwhelm me.

Given that it's a Wednesday with an away game tomorrow, practice should be getting out soon. Unless Coach dismissed everyone early.

I really don't fucking know.

The panic at seeing Graham is starting to settle in now. I've never had to deal with this before. The guy in Denver? It fizzled out on its own. No big dramatic breakup.

Maybe if there had been feelings involved, it might have been more difficult. It was just fun. Easy.

With Graham? It's a lot harder. Because feelings are definitely involved.

I follow my parents up from the garage, and with each passing floor, I wish I could have just waited in the car.

Like a coward.

When Dad unlocks the door, the apartment is empty. Blissfully so.

"Take a few minutes. We'll start packing," Dad tells me.

"Okay."

Walking in here now feels so different from that day all the months ago when I moved in here. Back then, it was more apprehension because I had no idea if Graham and I would get along well enough to make it work.

And now here we are.

The two of us in a weird limbo because I fell for him when I told myself I shouldn't. Because Graham was only just starting to figure out this side to him. A side that I've known about myself for as long as I've been alive.

Sitting down on the couch, the memories, while once happy, seem painful. Because I know what I have to do.

I can't keep Graham. It's clear he doesn't want me since he didn't come see me once in the hospital.

If he is going to figure out what he really wants—who he *really* is—then he needs to walk that path on his own. I don't want to unknowingly influence him in any way.

No matter how much it's going to suck.

Pushing up off the couch on my good hand, I head into my room to try and help my parents pack up my room.

"Do you want to pack everything up, Noah?" Mom asks. "Or is there anything we can leave and get later?"

"Just clothes for now. I don't think Graham will mind if I have to come back."

"We can always send Dad back to finish up later," she tells me.

"Just like that?" Dad laughs.

"I have school. And if we need someone to stay with Noah, we can have Piper stay for a few days."

"I think I can be by myself for a few hours."

We haven't even made it back to Denver, and I can feel the headache coming on of having people hovering twenty-four seven.

I love my parents, I really do, but there's a reason I don't live with them. Mom is muttering about my laundry not being folded properly while Dad just packs it up tight into a duffle.

Between the two of them—because I was yelled at when I tried to help—they make quick work of it. With the last few things being tossed in, there isn't much left to do.

Which means I might be able to take the coward's way out and not see Graham.

"I think this is everything?" Mom asks, looking around my now half-empty room.

"It's good enough for now." I left a lot of stuff in storage back in Denver because I didn't see the point in shipping it across the country when my place wasn't even ready. And after moving in with Graham, I didn't really need it. "If I need anything, I can just pick it up in Denver."

"Okay."

"I'll text the travel coordinator to let them know we'll be ready. Maybe we can grab you something to eat before the flight? Get some non-hospital food in you?" Dad asks.

"Sure."

It's then I hear the front door open.

"Do you want to see if Graham wants to come for dinner?" Dad asks.

I shake my head. "No. That's okay. I'd rather get back to Denver. But I might go talk to him for a few minutes."

Talking here? That I can handle. Probably.

Dinner with him? With my parents?

Abso-fucking-lutely not.

"We'll take everything down to the car and meet you out front. Take your time."

I nod at Dad as he and Mom heft the bags into their arms and head downstairs. I hear the pleasantries exchanged as I grab a Knights zip-up from my closet and slip into it.

I can't delay this anymore.

Heading out of my room, I find Graham standing in the living room by himself, looking at the back of the front door.

"Hey."

"You're leaving?" He spins on his heel to face me.

Graham looks about as good as I feel.

Which is to say, shit.

"I need someone to stay with me in case there's any relapse."

"Are they worried about that?"

Graham shoves his hands into his gray sweatpants. The sweatshirt he's wearing clings to his muscles. I hate how good he looks.

I hate that I know if we didn't have a game tonight, and I wasn't in this condition, that we'd probably be planning a fun night together.

I hate that this is what we've come to.

"It's a possibility."

"You can't stay here?"

The desperation in his voice is easy to pick up on. And it cracks my heart a little bit more.

"I can't. You know why."

"So you're going home? Were you even going to tell me?" Now there's bitterness in his voice. Not that I can blame him.

"I was planning on it."

"Really?" Graham crosses his arms. "Because I have a

feeling if I wasn't here right now, we wouldn't have crossed paths at all."

I rub a hand over my forehead. I don't want to be feeling any worse than I already am, but there's no denying it at this point.

"Graham—"

"Look." He holds out his hands. "I'm sorry. I didn't react well in the hospital, and I know that's on me."

"Is that why you didn't come see me?"

A few of the guys stopped by, but the one person I wanted to see—but also, didn't want to see at the same time—never actually came.

A shameful look comes over his face. I hate that I put it there, but really, he didn't come to see me.

"I didn't think you'd want to see me, to be honest."

"I wanted to." It comes out as a whisper. A wish that I wanted more than anything but also wouldn't have known how to deal with had he shown up.

"So stay." Graham takes one step closer but I take a step back. I can't say what I need to say if he's too close. Breathing Graham-infused air wouldn't do me any good right now.

"I think this thing between us has run its course."

"What?"

I nod, scrubbing a hand through my messy beard—*because who has time to shave in the fucking hospital?*

"We knew this wouldn't be a forever kind of thing, and now I have to focus on my recovery. I've got a long road ahead of me."

"That's it? You just decide that this is over and that's it?"

I shake my head and immediately regret it. Pushing the heel of my hand into my eyes, I try to stave off the wave of pain that settles there.

Fuck. Getting a concussion really sucks.

"Are you okay?"

Graham's voice is close. So close, I sink into the feel of it as it washes over me. Tears now sting my eyes.

I hate that I set myself up for this.

Graham was only just starting to explore his sexuality while I am secure in my own. It was never going to work. I let myself go down this road, and for what?

A broken heart and a banged-up head?

"I'll be fine," I whisper, keeping my eyes focused on my sneakers. "But I can't keep doing this, Graham."

"Tell me why."

"Because—"

"Look at me when you say it." Graham's knuckle comes under my chin as he drags my eyes up to meet his. The brown orbs are swirling with pain. The same pain I've been feeling every day for the last two weeks.

"Because we're in different places. I've never hidden who I am, and you're just figuring out who you are."

"But—"

I cut him off. "I don't want to pressure you. That's the absolute last thing that I want. But being here with you isn't going to make you figure it out any faster. And I can't keep doing this to myself."

Graham's warm hand cups my cheek. I want to lean into his touch but I don't. Everything hurts.

My head.

My shoulder.

My heart.

No need to make it worse than it is.

"I can be that person for you," Graham tells me. There's not much confidence infused in his tone, and it helps to solidify my decision.

"I don't want to force you into something you're not

ready for, Graham. I would never forgive myself if I did. I know what that guy's comment did to you."

"I wish it didn't."

I nod ever so softly. "I know. It's okay. I don't want you to get hurt in all of this."

Even though I know I'm breaking both of our hearts right now.

"I don't know when I'll be back, but I'll be sure to find another place when I do."

"I'm not kicking you out."

"I know, but I can't stay here."

Seeing Graham every day and not being able to touch him? It'd be a hell of my own making.

Leaning in, Graham presses a soft kiss to my lips. I want to savor it. Hold him close and let him press his mouth to every part of me that hurts. To make everything feel better.

Instead, I hold back the tears and step away from him. The man I have irrevocably fallen in love with.

"I'll see you around, Graham."

And with that, I'm gone.

Leaving my heart in the hands of a man who I wish could love me back.

Life fucking sucks.

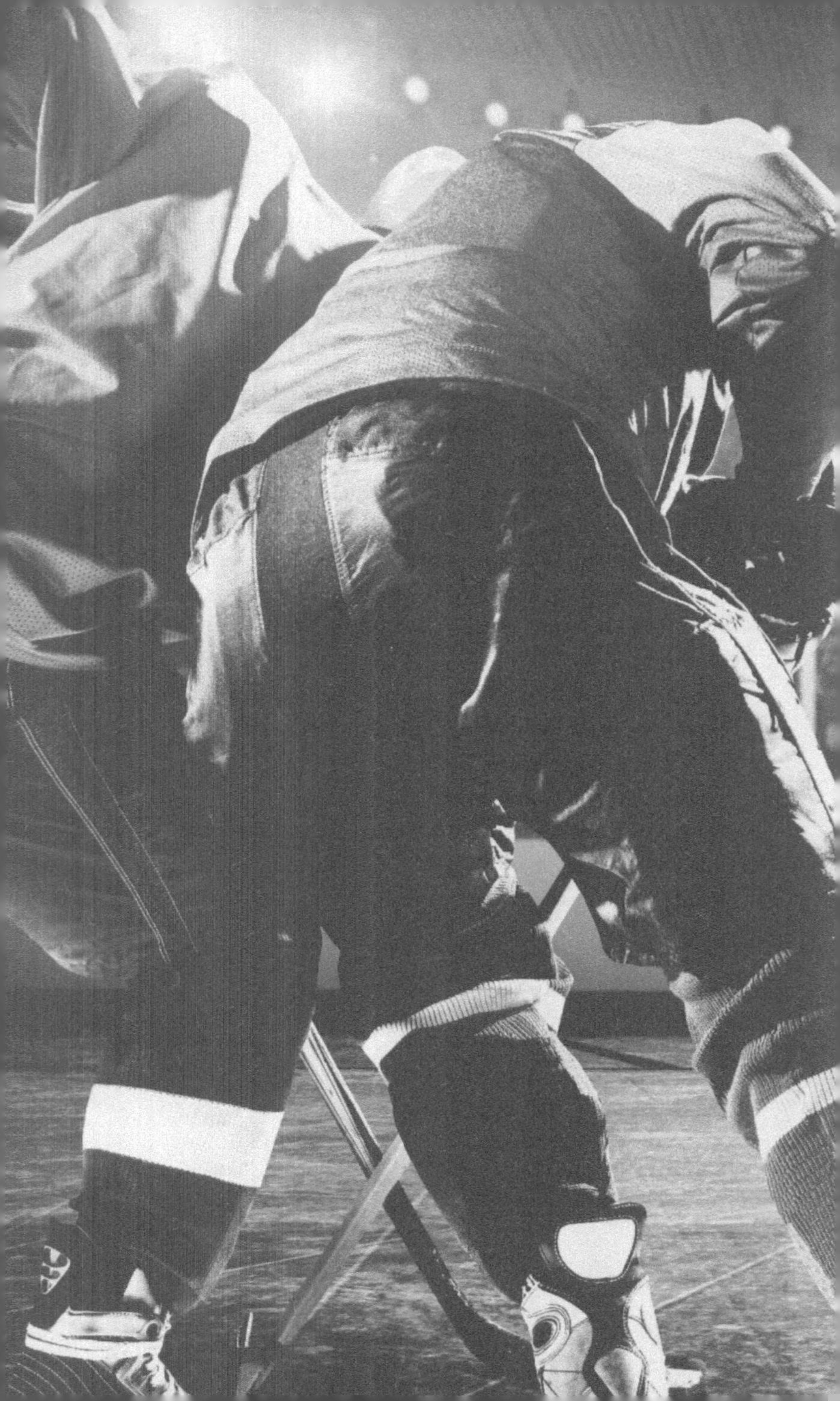

Chapter Twenty-Four

GRAHAM

"Nashville. Number ninety-eight. Two minutes for cross-checking."

"What the fuck is wrong with you?" Marcus shoves me toward the sin bin. "You're lucky they didn't toss you out of the game!"

"They're playing like assholes!" I shout back at Marcus, tugging at my helmet. "Maybe if they weren't such dicks!"

Raising my voice, I egg on the other team. I can't help myself. These last two weeks have been some of the worst of my playing career.

Cheap shots? I've been the king of them. Taking out my anger on anyone that crosses paths with me.

Boos rain down on me from the home crowd. Hard to blame them when I just gave the other team a power play.

"Get your head out of your ass, Fisher!" a fan shouts from behind me as the door shuts me into the tiny box. "You want them to beat us?"

I do my best to ignore the chirps and insults thrown my direction as play starts up again. I'm following the puck, watching our defensemen trying to block Dallas from getting into our zone. A few quick moves from one of their forwards and they've scored.

"Fuck." One well-timed goal and they're ahead of us. "Fuck."

I slam my stick against the boards before exiting the sin bin to even more boos. I can't remember a time when I've ever played this bad.

My head isn't in the game. It's the furthest thing from being here in our arena in Nashville. Hell, it's probably where my heart is right now.

In Denver.

Because ever since Noah left, things haven't been okay.

I've been half-assing practice, games…hell, even life. It feels like I'm skating through mud getting back to the bench.

An angry stare from the assistant coach greets me as he opens the door for me to take my spot on the bench.

"Get your head in the game, Fisher," Coach Andrews tells me as I grab my water bottle. "No more stupid penalties. We don't want to give them this game."

"Got it."

I take a swig as I watch the puck drop at center ice. Any other time, I'd be watching Noah take the puck.

With him gone, Dax has stepped up into his position.

And I fucking hate it.

It's Noah's starting spot, not Dax's. No matter how well he's doing, I want to go out there and rip it away from him. I don't care that we're on the same team. It's like I'm not supporting Noah by wanting him to do well.

This is why I haven't been able to keep my head on straight. It's been tied up with and about Noah. I can't keep going on like this.

"Fisher! You're up." The slap on my back has me flying over the boards and back into the action. For the next however many minutes I'm on the ice, I push every single thought out of my head.

It's not my best skating, but at least I manage not to draw another penalty. It's what allows me to push through the rest of the game as the Knights secure a win over Dallas.

No thanks to me.

The locker room is hopping. Every guy in here is ecstatic as Coach Andrews follows the last few guys into the room.

"That was a hard-fought win, gentlemen. We tried to give it to them a few times." I don't miss the subtle way Coach's eyes linger over me before moving on. "I know it was hard to lose a player of Noah's caliber, but I think we're doing a great job filling that void."

"We want to make him proud," someone pipes up from the other side of the locker room. I'm not sure who it is.

Hanging my head in shame, I stare down at my skates.

"I'm sure he is," Coach agrees. "I want to take this energy we're playing with down the stretch and maybe we might even be talking about playoffs. So rest up tonight, and we'll study film tomorrow then we'll work on cleaning up our mistakes. And let's not forget to congratulate Marcus, who will be heading to the All-Star game this weekend."

Cheers and claps echo around the locker room.

"Make sure to represent the Knights well," Coach Andrews tells him.

"You know I will."

He nods at him. "Finish it off for me."

Coach takes a step back as Marcus moves into the center of the locker room. "Alright, men. You heard him. Let's keep this going. Knights on three. One, two, three…"

"Knights!"

My voice doesn't carry the usual enthusiasm it has after a big win.

"Fisher. My office when you're done."

Coach doesn't even give me the chance to acknowledge him before he's out the door to where the coaches' offices are.

I can't keep going on like this. Just the thought of Noah has my heart clattering around in my chest. Something's got to give.

Being at home by myself is too hard. Everywhere I look, there are memories of me and Noah. Of better times. Of when he was still here and not back in Denver with his family.

Not with me.

Because that's not what we are to each other anymore.

"You doing okay?" Bode asks me, pulling me out of my errant thoughts. Thoughts that have been taking over every aspect of my life.

"Sorry. I'm just not with it."

Jasper comes up, clapping me on the shoulder. "Are you worried about Noah?"

"Uhh, yeah."

"He's going to be okay, right? Isn't that what the doctor said?" Bode asks.

"Yeah. Just hard to see a teammate go down like that."

"He'll bounce back. Come back better than ever next season," Jasper tells me. "He came back this season after that injury last year and look how good he was playing."

"Right."

No need to point out that the injury was at my hands, but I've had too much self-flagellation for one day.

"Playing like an asshole isn't going to help," Marcus chimes in. "I know it sucks, but the longer you're in the league, the greater chance it is you'll get injured."

"Is this supposed to make him feel better?" Jasper asks. "Because this isn't much of a pep talk, Cap."

Marcus rubs his nose, subtly flipping him off. "All I'm saying is, it happens. And the doctors said he'll make a full recovery. So why worry when he's going to be okay?"

Why worry?

If only I could tell these guys what is really bothering me. It's so much more than Noah's physical well-being.

It's my own well-being at stake too.

I don't want anyone else—man or woman. I want Noah Fields. Noah is the only person I've ever felt this way about. It's like I can't reconcile a way to be without him.

But I have to figure out a way to make it through the rest of the season without self-imploding. Wouldn't do anyone any good if I lost my position with the Knights. I'm still on a rookie contract and could be traded.

Which is the last thing I need if I want to be able to have a relationship with Noah.

Grabbing my towel, I hit the showers, wanting to get my conversation with Coach over and done with. I let the hot water stream down my body. It helps to calm the raging thoughts going through me.

Mainly what I'm going to say to Coach Andrews.

I wave to a few of the guys as they head out before I change back into my suit and head toward my reckoning.

The red carpet under my feet softens my footfalls. The windows looking into the other offices are dark, as most people have already cleared out after the game, likely going out to celebrate another great win.

I knock on the door, where Coach is waiting and calls me in.

A whiteboard takes up almost the entire wall to the right of me, with a desk piled high with papers. Coach Andrews is always studying our stats and other players' stats as well as looking for any edge he can get on any team we play. As any coach should do, but our old coach? Being a student of the game wasn't on his radar.

"Graham. Thanks for coming."

"You wanted to see me?"

I drop down into the seat across from him. Coach Andrews pulls off his thick glasses and drops them onto the desk in front of him.

"Is everything okay with you, Graham?"

Wiping my hands on my suit pants, I lean back in the chair. There's no point in lying to him. I'm clearly off my game. Anyone who knows anything can see that.

"I, uh, I guess I was a little more shaken up about the hit Noah took than I let on."

"It's okay that you were. A lot of the guys were. But you need to talk to us about these things."

"I guess our old coach didn't really let us express our feelings."

Coach Andrews shakes his head. "Look. I know a lot of people still frown upon men having feelings, but something traumatic happened, and I want you to feel you can come to me."

"Okay."

"And not go after other players to take out whatever you're feeling."

That has a chagrined smile spreading across my face. "I know. I haven't been at my best."

"Do you need some time off? It's okay if you're not doing okay."

"No!" I bark out, a little too loudly. "Sorry, Coach. I'll get my head back in the game. No more dumb mistakes."

"We need you, Graham. You've been an asset to this team from the beginning, and I'd hate to see that change because of something that is out of your control."

"I'm sorry, Coach. I promise, I'll get my head back in the game."

"Is that it? Nothing else is bothering you?" He twirls the pen in his hand around his fingers, studying me.

I shake my head. "No, Coach. That's all. I'll make sure tonight won't happen again."

"Good. And you know my door is always open should you need to talk about anything."

"I know. Thanks, Coach."

"Get out of here. I'll see you for practice tomorrow."

"See ya."

I don't waste another minute before bolting out of his office and running out of the arena. I'm not in the mood to be stopped again and asked about my performance tonight.

Chapter Twenty-Five

NOAH

"Even with the loss of the Black Diamonds' star player last season, Noah Fields, the team is looking better than ever. Paddack has stepped in and filled his skates with a fervor any team could hope for."
"I wasn't sure what Bexley Hart was thinking when she traded for him, but she saw something the rest of us didn't. Of course you never like to see a player of Fields's caliber go down, but Paddack will be a fine young player for Colorado for years to come."

Of course. The analysts calling tonight's game don't know the knife they're digging into my chest. I can see with my own eyes what a strong player Paddack has become since joining the Black Diamonds. With Hollins and Williams as captain and alternate captain, they're about the best damn players he could learn from.

Not that I hadn't been contributing in Nashville. The team has been playing with a renewed intensity. So much so, that we might even have a shot at making the playoffs.

It seems no team needs me.

I'm wallowing. I know it. But I've been cooped up at my parents' house for two weeks, and it's about a week too long.

Even though I've been cleared to not be under concussion watch twenty-four seven, I don't have anywhere else to go considering I sold my house before I moved to Nashville.

Except I'm still being hovered over all the time.

"Do you need anything, sweetheart?" Mom asks, coming into the living room and smoothing my hair back from my forehead.

If not her, it's my dad.

"I'm fine."

"Are you?" She comes around the couch and has her arms crossed in front of her. "You've been moping on the couch since you got home."

"I have not."

"Then why am I here?" comes my sister's voice from behind me.

Turning toward her, I see Piper dropping her purse and coat on the kitchen table before coming into the living room and standing next to my mom.

"I don't know. Why are you here and not at the game?"

The TV has been on with the low drone of the Black Diamonds game playing in the background. Even though I no longer play for them, I still watch them. I have too many friends there not to. Family, really.

"Because Mom didn't want you by yourself tonight," Piper tells me.

"Where are you going?" I ask our mom. With the two of them standing together like this, they look eerily similar. Piper has always been the spitting image of her, but with the way her arms are crossed, it's like I'm looking at two of my mother. "Also, this is freaky. The two of you like this."

Neither of them say anything, but they both quirk a brow at me like I'm the problem.

"Call me if you need me, dear." Mom drops a kiss on Piper's cheek. She points a stern finger at me. "Don't watch too much TV."

"Yes, Mother." I roll my eyes at her—like the moody teenager I feel like I am right now—as she kisses the top of my head and heads out, ignoring my question as to where she's going.

"Seriously. Why are you moping?" Piper smacks my leg as she takes a spot directly next to me on the oversized couch. I can feel her eyes on me.

"Shouldn't you be at the game?" I point to the TV.

"I'm good."

Piper's engagement ring glints in the low light of the room. Even though it's been a few weeks, harsh lighting can still give me a headache. The TV? I'm listening to it more than watching. Of course Colorado is dominating.

Nothing new. I turn my attention away from my sister and look up at the ceiling, closing my eyes.

I hate how everyone is constantly worried about me. The hovering. The asking how I'm feeling. I know they're doing it out of love, but I hate it.

Because I can't really tell them how I'm feeling. Even though they're sensing that it's more than the injury and being benched.

How can I tell them I'm in love with someone who isn't out? That I broke my own rule and started something with Graham when I knew better?

Maybe I should talk to Piper about it. I mean, it's not like I have to tell her who it is.

"Can I ask you something?" I turn my head to face her, and it's hard to ignore the gleeful look on her face. I can count on one hand the number of times I've asked her for advice. With her being younger than me by a few years, I never really went to her.

"Sure."

"What do you do when you're in love with someone you can't have?"

"You're in love?" Now she looks shocked.

"I think so?"

Piper pins me with a look so like our mother, it pulls a smile out of me. One of the only ones that I've given out lately.

"How do you think so?"

I scrub a hand over my forehead. "I've never been in love before, Piper. It's a new thing for me. I was just fine with the guys on the side during the season, but when I found someone, I started something knowing it wouldn't last."

"Why can't it last?" Piper asks.

"He's not out." I blow out a breath. "I'd never force him to come out, but we're in different places in our life. He's still figuring out who he is. Why would he want to be tied down to me?"

"Hey!" Piper looks like she's going to punch me in the arm, but thinks better of it. Good thing I'm still in this sling, because she packs a fierce punch. "Any guy would be lucky to have you. And maybe you're going about this all wrong. Maybe he just needs time to figure out who he is."

"I don't want to push him into anything he doesn't want. So until then—"

"You're moping on the couch. Been there."

Piper and Cash went through a rough patch thanks to

Piper's ex and his girlfriend at the time. Thankfully they were able to move past it, because as different as the two of them are, they are perfect together.

"It really fucking sucks," I confirm.

"Can you tell me who it is?" Piper asks.

"I want to, but I can't."

I wish I could, because maybe she could say something that would make it better. But I wouldn't do that to Graham. It's not my thing to tell. To out him.

All I've done is think about this man for the last two weeks. The quiet moments together in hotel rooms across the country. The night at the bar. Hell, even the pain in his eyes when I left.

That one hurts the most to think about.

I don't know when I gave my heart to Graham, and I don't know if I'll ever get it back. He knows what this life is like. Maybe that's why I fell for him. I was just fine these last few years being on my own. I didn't feel like my life was missing anything.

Watching the guys around me fall in love didn't affect me.

Not until Graham.

I guess all it takes is finding the right person. Who knew the right person for me would be the guy that injured me and got me traded to Nashville?

"I'm sorry, Noah. There's nothing worse than a broken heart."

"It fucking sucks."

The two of us sit together, watching the game. Piper keeps her cheers to a reasonable volume as Cash scores a goal. Watching the game like this, he makes it look easy.

"If it isn't my two favorite kids," Dad's voice rings out in the living room.

"Why aren't you out with Mom?" Piper asks.

"She's out with Peyton and Frankie tonight." Dad takes the seat opposite us, kicking his feet up on the ottoman. "How you feeling?"

Don't roll your eyes, Noah. Don't roll your eyes.

"He's fine, Dad. I'm taking care of him," Piper answers for me.

"What she said."

"Just leave him be, Dad. Noah is getting tired of everyone hovering."

"Oh he is?" Dad asks Piper, quirking a brow in her direction.

"Yes." Piper nods at him.

"And are you answering for him?" Dad shifts his focus to me.

"She is." I laugh.

Dad rolls his eyes at us and turns to watch the game. "I can't remember the last time you two ganged up on me, and I don't like how long it's been."

"Blame Noah for moving away."

"Hey, it's not like I asked to be traded." I shift away from Piper and glare at both of them.

"You still don't come home enough. Your mom misses you," Dad tells me.

"Just Mom?" I raise a brow at him. "Or you too?"

"We both miss you. You could at least call more often." He pins me with the same look. "Shouldn't take a concussion to get you to come home."

"Okay, you got me there. But you know my schedule during the season."

Dad stands. "I know. You guys want anything to drink?"

"Old-fashioned, please," Piper says.

"Just water."

Piper watches as Dad heads into the kitchen. "You

know, you could come stay with me and Cash. At least until you go back to Nashville."

"Think you could take a few days off and help me find a place to live?"

"I thought you were staying with Graham?" Piper looks confused.

"It was only temporary. I'll need my own place once I get back."

"Wait…" Piper has the look of someone trying to piece something together.

Shit. Did I give too much away? There's no way. I haven't even come close to hinting at who the guy is.

Except I must have given my sister just enough because her face lights up.

"Oh my God! It's him!"

"Shh!" I hush her as Dad comes into the living room and hands us each our drink.

"What are you two whispering about?" he asks.

"Dad, could you maybe grab us some pretzels?"

"Okay?" he asks, confused more than anything.

"Thank you." She watches as he leaves before turning her attention back to me. "It's Graham, right?"

"Piper, seriously! Stop talking!"

"That means I'm right." The look of gloating on Piper's face is too much for me.

"Okay, I'm going to watch the game in the silence of my room."

"Hey." She grabs my arm and tugs me back down onto the couch. "Look, I won't say anything. Trust me, but it makes sense."

"It does?" Am I really that transparent?

"Yes. The way you've always grumbled about him and what he did to you. You hated him. Only makes sense you fell in love."

"Have you always been this smart?" I ask, tongue-in-cheek.

"Yes. You just ignored your little sister," Piper says with a cocky smile. "I only call it like I see it."

"Like I said, it fucking sucks."

Chapter Twenty-Six

GRAHAM

"You want anything for dinner?" Mom asks.

"I'm okay."

"You sure?" She ruffles my hair, drawing my attention to her.

"I'm good."

The All-Star game plays quietly in the background in the living room. Dad is in the kitchen behind us cooking.

Not much has changed about this place since I left. The shelves lining the wall next to the TV are stuffed to the brim with pictures. Pictures from football games. Super Bowls. Me at hockey practice. Holidays with families.

The walls of this house are filled with nothing but love.

Something I haven't felt a lot of these last few weeks.

It's been a weird time for me. Ever since Noah came back here, to Denver, it's like I've been in a fog. A quiet, ever-present fog without Noah at home.

I didn't want him to live with me, but now, it's not the same without him. I've been spending more and more time training at the rink. The one upside? I'm in the best shape of my life.

And it's helped the Knights get on a winning streak for one of the first times in a long time, so I'll keep doing it.

"You sure you don't want dinner, Graham?" Dad calls from the kitchen.

"I'm not hungry."

"I'm making your favorite stir-fry."

Damn. It does smell good. "I guess I could eat."

Both of them are in the kitchen, getting dinner ready, the two of them working together like a well-oiled machine.

It brings another pang to my heart. Is this what I could have had with Noah if I weren't too scared to be out? That singular thought has been plaguing me.

But how in the world can I do that when I'm not even out to the two people who are the most important people in my world?

"You've been quiet." Dad hands me a plate before I walk over to the dining room table.

"Just tired. You know this late in the season that everything hurts."

Dad laughs. "I still can't bend my knees without them hurting."

"Your knees are just fine," Mom tells him as she sits down next to me.

The two of them bicker back and forth over the kind of shape my dad is in as I shovel dinner into my mouth.

Fuck. I really did need a good home-cooked meal. That's the one thing I'm terrible at—cooking for myself. With needing to fine-tune my nutrition during the season, I use the team's nutritionist to help me plan everything out.

So getting to have my favorite meal at home is a brief reprieve from the shit going on in my own head.

"Are you okay?" Mom asks, clearing the dirty dishes

and setting them in the sink. Her warm brown eyes—the same as mine—are staring me down.

It's the look that always had me spilling my guts when I was in high school. Maybe it's why she is such a good coach. She doesn't let anyone hold on to any shit that's in their heads.

Back then, I hated it. Now though? Maybe this is the time I should be talking to them about everything that's turning me inside out.

"Uhh, can I talk to you and Dad?"

I wipe my hands on my sweats and stand, walking around the table. The two of them share a panicked look. "Oh God, is everything okay? Are you hurt? Being traded? What is it?"

Mom pulls out one of the stools at the counter and drops down into it. Dad is standing right next to her with an equally fearful look on his face.

"It's nothing like that."

"Then what is it, Graham?" Dad asks. "You know you can tell us anything."

"I think I'm gay," I blurt out.

Well, I guess ripping off the Band-Aid is the way to do it.

"Gay?" Mom asks from her seat, slightly stunned.

"Well, bi."

"How did you come to this realization?" Dad asks, dropping down onto his forearms, leaning closer to me. He's the same height as Mom like this.

And glancing between the two of them now, my nerves are close to spilling out of me. I'm a spitting image of my dad. But I have the same eyes as my mom.

"Well, I had—"

Mom slaps her hand over my mouth. "If you love me, you will not finish that sentence."

"What?" I mumble against it.

"I don't want to hear about your sex life."

"Eww. Why would I tell you about that?" I shudder at the thought.

"Because you're a Fisher. You overshare."

"Hey, we do not!" Dad denies.

"Have you met your mother?" Mom says, turning to look at him. "I do not want to hear about her sex life, but I hear about it regularly. *Regularly*, Knox."

"Whoa!" Both of us cover our ears.

"See?" She quirks a brow at us. "Your fault."

"I'm not an oversharer."

"Still your genes. I had to hear all about your mother's new boyfriend and how her old one gave the new woman herpes."

"Can I burn my ears off?" Dad groans.

"We're getting off track," I interrupt.

"Sorry, Graham. We're listening." Mom reaches out and takes my hand in hers. "I promise, we won't interrupt."

"Uhh…" I scrub a nervous hand over the back of my neck. "It just kind of happened. I didn't really plan on it, but I met someone who kind of changed the way I saw myself."

"We love you," Mom tells me, reaching out and grabbing my free hand. "No matter what. Whoever you love, it doesn't matter. I hope you know that."

"I know." It's still nice to hear though.

Mom opens her arms and I fall into them in a hug I didn't know I needed. "Is this what has you so torn up? Telling us?"

"No," I mumble.

"Then what is it?" Dad asks, squeezing my shoulder.

"I'm in love with Noah."

"Noah? Noah *Fields* Noah?" Dad asks.

"One and the same."

"Wow."

"Does Noah know this?" Mom asks.

"No."

"So what's the problem then?" Dad asks. "Can't you just tell him how you feel?"

"That's the problem. I don't know how to be out with him. I'm scared."

I hate how small my voice sounds when I tell them my biggest fear.

"Oh, my sweet boy." Mom presses a kiss to the top of my head. "I don't think anyone can decide that for you."

"You know, Alex could help," Dad tells me.

"Really?" I pull out of Mom's arms and look over at him.

"Of course. He can't make the decision for you, but he struggled with it before he came out."

I don't know why I didn't think of it before. It goes to show just how in my head I've really been. But I also don't know if I would have talked to him without talking to my parents first.

"Okay, yeah. I'll talk to Uncle Alex. Maybe that will help."

I DON'T KNOW if I've ever been so nervous in my life. Not even before my first NHL game. This is a whole different kind of nervous that I'm feeling.

Until the front door swings open.

"Are you going to stand out here all day, or are you going to ring the doorbell?"

Uncle Carter is standing in the open doorway with a smile on his face. Thin glasses rest on his nose, gray peppering his blond hair. He's in a Black Diamonds sweatshirt as he pulls the door open even farther, welcoming me.

"Sorry. I was just trying to work up the courage to knock."

"C'mon in, Graham."

"Thanks. I was hoping Uncle Alex might be here?"

"He is. Let me get him for you."

I follow him in and take a seat in the living room. I've been here more times than I can count growing up. Our families were always close, even after all of them stopped playing.

I sink into the oversized couch as Carter heads to where I know the office in the house is. It gives my nerves time to multiply. Maybe I'm not as ready for this as I thought.

But the thought of bolting is pushed from my head when they come back in the room.

"Graham. How are you?" Uncle Alex walks into the room with a smile on his face. He's in a sweatshirt almost identical to Carter's, and it brings a smile to my face at how similar these two are. "Enjoying the All-Star break?"

I stand, accepting the hug he gives me. "Definitely a nice break."

"Glad to hear it. So, what brings you here?"

"I'll let you two talk," Carter tells us, dropping a kiss on Alex's cheek.

"Actually, I could talk to you both."

They exchange a look before they both take a seat on the couch. I sit down opposite them, trying to quell my nerves.

"I wanted to talk to you about something."

You can do this, Graham. I have to keep telling myself that so I don't chicken out.

"I, umm, I think I'm bi," I start. "Well, no. I am."

"Okay." Alex takes hold of Carter's hand, resting their joined hands on his lap.

He doesn't push, just giving me the space to get out what I need to tell them.

"This is a new thing. The last few months, really. And now that I've found this person, I'm trying to come to terms with my sexuality and how to be out so I can be with him. Because he's out and I'm, well, not."

Uncle Carter leans forward, glancing at Alex before turning to face me. "Is this person pressuring you to come out? Because you shouldn't come out for anyone but yourself."

I shake my head. "He's not, no. But I realize I love him and want to be with him."

"And you're scared," Alex clarifies.

"Yes."

"The terrifying feeling of being in love," Carter says. "It's not easy."

"It's hard to decide when the time is right for you to come out," Alex starts. "I stayed in the closet for too long, terrified that coming out would get me ousted from the league. It's the last thing I wanted, and honestly? I was scared. But then I realized that the time was never right because I hadn't yet found the right person to be with."

The tender look they share has my heart clanging around against my rib cage. Could Noah and I have this? It's what I want more than anything.

"What if it doesn't work out? What if the guys on the team aren't accepting? What if—"

"Graham." Alex holds a hand up, cutting me off. "Life is nothing but what-ifs. We have no idea if things will work out or not. That's why you need to do this for you. Not for anyone else. When I came out, I did it knowing full well I might never see Carter again. But just because I came out, doesn't mean it's always easy. There were some hard days, but it was easier having him at my side."

"It was," Carter agrees. "It takes a great deal of strength to come out when you're in the public spotlight. No matter what, someone is going to have an opinion about it, even with how far we've come for LGBTQIA+ people in sports. *You* have to weigh whether the attention you'll inevitably get will be worth it or not. It's okay if you're not ready. You don't have to do it just because you feel like you have to. Know that, Graham. No one is forcing you to come out."

I blow out a breath, leaning back into the couch. I can't make this decision with anyone but me in mind. I know that. I *knew* that. Having these two reiterate it to me makes it that much harder to come to terms with what I'm thinking of doing.

I love Noah. I know this. It's been the only thing I've been thinking about for the last few weeks. I honestly thought the feelings I had toward him would go away. That it would have been a fling that I got out of my system.

That is so far from the truth that it's laughable.

Now I'm here at my uncles' house trying to figure out what I want to do next. Do I keep my truth hidden? Do I take the time to fully figure it out before revealing whatever it might be?

Or do I fly by the seat of my pants and say fuck it and come out to everyone?

"Coming out looks different to everyone," Alex says.

"Are you reading my mind?" I laugh.

He gives me a warm smile. "You don't have to make some big proclamation to the world. I did what I felt was best for me. If you decide you do want to come out, you get to decide how you do it."

"Really?"

"Really," they say at the same time.

"I guess in my position I thought it would be all or nothing."

"Have you talked to your parents? That might be a good place to start," Alex tells me. "Your dad was nothing but supportive when I came out."

I smile back at them, feeling at ease for the first time. "I did. They were the ones who told me to come talk to you."

"Have we helped or made it even worse for you?"

I stand, letting them know I don't want to take up any more of their time. "Helped. A lot, actually."

"Good." Alex wraps me in a hug as we walk to the door.

"Thank you. I appreciate you talking it out with me."

Carter gives me a hug as Alex opens the door for me. "We're here if you need to talk more. Whatever you need, day or night."

"Thanks."

Stepping outside, I take a deep breath of the cold, Denver air. I know exactly what I need to do. The decision comes easily.

No nerves. No overthinking it.

Just do it.

Chapter Twenty-Seven

NOAH

"Is it weird to be here?" Piper asks, getting out of the car in the VIP parking lot.

"Would you quit asking me that?" I groan.

When Piper said she would take me to my appointment today and then to the game tonight, I figured she'd be the best option. No nagging like my mom.

"If I could smack you, I would." Piper rolls her eyes at me. "I have not asked you once. Just because Mom and Dad are being overbearing, doesn't mean you have to take it out on me."

"Fuck. I'm sorry, Piper."

I wrap my arm around her shoulders, and we flash our badges to the security guard and head inside. It's nice that the security guard looks new and I don't recognize him. As much as I love the people in this building, I want to make it to the family suite without having to be stopped every few feet.

"You're lucky I love you, Noah. Otherwise I would not have brought you here and made you ride with everyone else."

Since the Knights are in town, my dad and all his old playing buddies, plus their spouses, will all be in attendance. I haven't seen many of them since I got home, opting to hide out in my room under the guise of healing.

Tonight? I'll be under the microscope, so the less time with them, the better.

By the time we get to the suite, Piper bounds over to greet the host like an old friend. Wearing her fiancé's jersey, she fits in well here.

A few of the players' spouses are here, some I recognize and some I don't.

Angie is already here, walking over to greet me.

"Hey, stranger."

"Hey." I wrap her and her growing baby bump in a hug. "How you feeling?"

"Good, but I should be asking you the same thing."

"Okay."

"Yeah?" she asks, rubbing a hand over her stomach. "Piper says it's been a hard few weeks."

"Just getting used to not playing. That's all."

Even though it has been a hard few weeks, and Piper knows more about the why than anyone else—the only other person besides me and Graham—I know she wouldn't have told anyone else. She's one of the people I trust most in my life.

"I know your team misses you. Troy and the guys do too. Make sure you call them while you're home, okay?"

"Yes, Mom." I laugh.

"Hey. Gotta get some practice while I can."

"You'll be a great mom."

I've known Angie as long as I've been alive. When Nick came along, she loved showing him off to everyone she met. Babied him within an inch of his life.

She was born to be a mother.

"Thanks. We're ready."

"And I'm ready to be an honorary aunt." Piper walks over to us.

"He'll be here soon enough."

"If it isn't the apples of our eyes."

Turning my head, I watch as the number of people in the suite nearly triples with the arrival of our families.

"Wait. Why aren't you wearing your brace?" Mom asks, immediately zeroing in on the fact that my right arm is no longer locked to my body in the contraption that I've been wearing for the last few weeks. Leave it to her eagle eye to notice it before anything else.

"Cleared to not have to wear it anymore."

The look on her face is one of relief. "That's great, sweetheart."

"One step closer," Dad tells me. "Keep doing what you're doing."

"I will."

Uncle Alex, standing beside my dad, is studying me, and I squirm a bit under his gaze. With glasses hiding his eyes, I have no idea what he's thinking.

"How are you doing otherwise, Noah?"

"I'm doing fine. Thanks."

I can't tell you the number of times I've muttered that I'm fine in the last few weeks. Or good. All to get people to stop hovering. Now that the doctor has cleared me to increase my workouts and not wear a brace, I feel like I'll have more of a leg to stand on when I tell them I am *fine*.

"Good. We're all here for you if you need it."

"I know." I really shouldn't be ungrateful. Not when I have so many people in my corner. "I appreciate it."

"I won't ask how you're doing since you're doing so fine," Knox tells me with a smirk on his face.

Seeing him might be the hardest of all. All because he

reminds me of what I don't have. Graham is a spitting image of his dad.

I miss him. I hate how much I do.

"The finest of fines." I laugh.

"Good." Knox claps me on the back. "Keep it that way and you'll be back with the Knights in no time."

"Not too soon." A new voice enters the fray of people lingering in the suite around the food tables. One I recognize well as soon as her face pops up. "I wouldn't mind you being out to make it easier for my boys."

"Bexley. It's nice to see you." I extend my hand out to her. "I wish I could be out there to beat them."

"I know you do." She smiles at me. "I wish you were out there. It's a shame what happened."

"I'm getting better."

Bexley nods at me. She exudes a warmth that makes me see why Nick fell for her so easily. "I hope you do. The Knights won't be the same until you get back out there."

"I appreciate that."

"Now if you'll excuse me, I have to go encourage my team to be the ones to win tonight." Bex winks at me in a playful manner.

Having been with the Black Diamonds for most of my playing career, I know she likes to be in the locker room prior to the game. She was always down there encouraging us. Hyping us up to play our best.

Bexley really was the best GM I've played for. Nashville's is great, I can't deny that, but Bexley really does love her team, and it's evident in everything she does for them.

"Nice seeing you, Bex."

"You too. Good to see you on your feet."

She's out the door, and before someone else can come talk to me, I take my place in the back corner of the two rows of seats that overlook the ice. Both teams are out there warming up.

This is the first time I've been in an arena since my injury.

The sounds of the crowd.

The skates on the ice.

The cold air, the smell of hockey—that smell that you can't describe but any hockey fan would know—goes a long way to soothe the constant ache in my bones.

It settles me in a way that nothing else has been able to lately. It reinvigorates my drive to be able to get back out on the ice. To push all the wayward thoughts of this being the end for me out of my head.

The normal pregame routine starts, amping up the crowd. It's something I've never gotten to experience like this. I've always been down with the team. The home crowd is rocking, and when the Knights are announced, the boos are so loud, it could trigger the Richter scale.

My eyes trail over every guy on the ice—purposefully avoiding Graham—and they look good. Ready. Even though I can't be down there on the ice, I know they're ready.

We've been talking about this game all season. About wanting to beat the Black Diamonds again, this time on their turf and when it matters more than the preseason game played at a neutral site. It was a good win. But this one? It would be huge for us.

The game starts and the crowd settles down around us.

"Nick is looking good," Piper tells me, dragging a carrot through her hummus before crunching down on it. "He's really worked hard to up his game this season."

"Our guys will beat him. Just you wait." My voice is cocky. I know we have what it takes to beat this team. I want it so bad, I can taste it.

"You sure about that?" Piper asks. "Reigning cup champs. That last win was a fluke."

I shake my head at her. "You know that doesn't matter season to season. The Knights are good. Not a fluke, sis."

"Uh-oh. Fields siblings are getting snippy." Colin laughs. "I don't know who I'm placing my money on."

"I do," I say confidently. "Knights are winning."

Piper sets her plate on her lap and turns to face me. "Alright. What are we betting? I'm taking the Black Diamonds. Obviously."

"Loser has to pick up the tab when we go out to celebrate our victory."

Piper holds out her hand to shake. "You're on. But not just my drinks, the team's drinks too."

"Hope you're ready to lose." I squeeze her hand harder than necessary, but hey, it's what siblings do.

"Not a chance."

There's a smug look on Piper's face that I hope the Knights wipe away at the end of the game. Play is fairly even during the first period, and early on in the second until Marcus gets a breakaway and is able to put the puck in the back of the net.

"Yes!" I jump up, mindful not to throw up my arm while it's still healing, and cheer my team on. "That was a thing of beauty."

"Yeah, yeah," Piper dismisses me. "Easy. We'll get it back."

The Knights do a great job at keeping the Black Diamonds at bay, but only for so long. A loose scramble for the puck ends up past our goalie, evening the score.

By the time the third period starts, play is starting to get chippy. With the score staying at 1-1, each team is looking for whatever advantage they can find.

"Knights are looking good." Alex drops down into the

seat in front of me and turns around. "Looks like Coach Andrews has done a lot of good for the team."

"He has." I sip on my water. "I hope I get to play with him for a lot longer."

"A good coach can make or break a team. You're lucky you didn't have to play with their old coach. I never heard great things about him."

"Graham wasn't a fan of his," Knox says as he takes the seat next to him. "But what can you do? You have to play the hand you're dealt."

The two of them start chatting together as the Black Diamonds head toward our goalie. He deflects the pass with ease and it's Graham picking it up.

"C'mon. C'mon."

Graham is flying down the ice. His puck control is flawless as he fires off a slap shot toward Nick, and it flies right past his shoulder and lights the lamp.

"Yes!"

Fuck. That goal was a thing of beauty, putting us in the lead against one of the best teams in the league. My old team.

Alex is congratulating Knox after the goal as the guys swarm Graham on the ice. If I were on the ice, I'd be down there. Right in the thick of it.

Thinking of how we would be celebrating later if that were the case has a dull ache settling in my gut. Because that is not going to happen anymore.

I push it away, trying to keep the energy up for the team as they battle it out for the last few minutes. The home crowd is trying to get the Black Diamonds back into it, staying on their feet for the rest of the game to try and even the score. Even when they pull Nick from goal, it's a fruitless effort.

The Knights beat the Black Diamonds 2-1.

"Hell yes!"

The guys are clapping each other on the helmets before heading off the ice. It was a hard-fought win against one of the best teams in the league. The Knights looked fucking amazing out there. Sure, there are things we need to clean up, but that's how most games go.

Piper saunters up to me, her arms crossed and an annoyed look on her face. "Pretty proud of yourself," she tells me.

"The guys looked fucking awesome out there." I can't hide my excitement for them. "C'mon. You have to be a little excited that your brother's team won."

"After you beat my fiancé's team? We'll see."

I don't miss the smile on her face as she turns to head back into the suite.

The feeling of victory is something I'm used to in this building. I thought it would be harder to see my team win without me on the ice, but it wasn't.

It felt amazing to see all of their hard work pay off. We still have a long way to go if we want to make it to the playoffs, but the Knights have a bright future ahead.

One that I'm ready to play an active role in as soon as I'm in shape again.

"I don't think I've seen you this happy in a long time." Dad comes over to my spot in the suite and stands next to me. "It's nice."

"I know I wasn't out there for the win, but I felt like I was a part of it, you know?"

Dad nods. "I know the feeling. It's still your team out there and you want them to do well."

"Doesn't hurt we beat my old team."

I never would have heard the end of it if they beat us. At least I can rub it in their faces when I see them.

"That's the spirit."

The stands are emptying around us as I take some time to savor this moment.

"You know, Dad, over the last few seasons, I was really starting to wonder if I was more harm than good to my team."

"Noah—"

"No, I'm serious," I interrupt him. "It seems like I've been riding the bench more than I've been on the ice, but maybe it just means I'm moving in a different direction. That I can help coach my team and help the younger players learn more than just being the star."

"That's a good attitude to have. The team wouldn't have put you on IR if they didn't care about you as a player. I can attest to that more than anyone."

"Don't get me wrong. I wish I could be out there with the guys, but maybe I'm up here for a reason."

What that reason is, I'm still figuring out. But at least I'm starting to get my sanity back and not be so tied up in the fact that I'm not playing right now.

"I'm going to head down and see the team."

"Want me to go with you?" Piper asks.

I shake my head. "No. Go see Cash. I'll be fine."

"You sure?"

"Go." I push Piper in the opposite direction of me. "I promise, I'm good. Break the news to Cash that you're buying all of us drinks."

Piper rolls her eyes at me before dropping a kiss on my cheek. "Even if Cash doesn't win, I'm still happy your team won. Because I want you to win another cup too."

"Really?" I ask.

"Really. But try not to beat Colorado for it, okay?"

"No promises." I laugh.

Following everyone out of our suite, I take a few deep

breaths. I want to see the guys. Congratulate them on their big win.

Seeing Graham though? I haven't seen him since I left our place in Nashville. Well, his place. Do I want to see him?

At this point, I feel like I can see him and it won't rip me in half.

I only hope he wants to see me too.

Chapter Twenty-Eight

The crowd noise is frenetic. With each passing second, it gets louder and louder in here, the fans encouraging their team to get the puck in the goal to tie the game.

Even pulling Nick from goal doesn't do the trick.

But as time ticks away, the final horn sounds.

Knights 2, Black Diamonds 1.

"Hell yeah!" Jasper comes skating over and jumps on top of me as we start celebrating on Colorado's ice. "That was fucking amazing!"

"I can't believe we just pulled off the upset!" Bode tackles us, pushing us farther into the boards. Fans are pounding their annoyance out on the glass, but I couldn't care less.

Euphoria takes over at the feeling of beating this team. A team that we've now beat twice when no one said we could do it. But here we are at the end of the game having come out on top.

"That goal was a thing of beauty, Flounder." Marcus holds out his gloved fists for a bump. "Fucking amazing!"

"Fuck, that felt good."

"Fucking great." Bode claps me on the back.

We leave the ice and head back down the tunnel toward our locker room. The arena is quiet compared to when we arrived. I love that we shut the crowd down.

It felt fucking amazing.

"Fuck yeah!" Dax cheers out as I enter the visitors' area. "I can't believe we beat the defending Stanley Cup champions!"

I don't know if I've ever been in a locker room that has been so boisterous following a win. It's the Knights biggest win to date.

"What a play by Fisher in the third!" Coach Andrews pipes up as he hops up onto one of the chairs that line the wall. "That was a thing of beauty! Way to keep your head in the game."

A furious blush creeps up my neck at Coach's words. I know the meaning behind them. Hell, so does most of the team.

If I didn't get my head on straight, we might not have had this win. The setup was perfect—I was able to intercept the pass from Hollins to Williams and block what might have been a sure-fire goal. With the caliber of players those two are, it would've been hard to stop.

But with the stop late in the third period with time winding down, they weren't able to put the biscuit in the basket.

Earning a hard-fought win for the Knights.

"Highlight reel for sure." Jasper claps me on the back.

"Felt really good," I call out.

"Looked even better from up above."

That voice. It has nerves boiling up inside that threaten to explode out of me.

I haven't seen Noah since he left me standing in my condo almost a month ago. A day hasn't gone by when I haven't thought of him.

"Noah. Just trying to take the lead from what you've shown us."

My eyes dart up, scanning the locker room to find him in a hug with Coach Andrews. The guys start swarming him, but I'm rooted to the spot. My feet won't budge.

Because it's him. Noah.

When he left Nashville, he looked dazed. It's like he wasn't quite all there. I know it was because of the concussion, but maybe it was also because of me.

Now? Now, it looks like he has a clear head. His eyes are brighter.

Fuck. I didn't realize how desperate I was to get even the slightest look at him.

"It hasn't been the same without you."

"We've missed you, man."

I hang back as the guys crowd around him. There's so much that I want to say to him, but I don't know where to start.

I'm sorry?

I miss you?

I love you?

The only reason I know how he's doing is because of my dad. The crowd around him starts to disperse, and that's when our eyes finally meet.

Taking the first steps toward him, I have no idea what I'm going to say.

Until someone else is calling for me.

"Fisher. Press wants to talk to you," Coach Mickey yells out to me.

Guess I have a reprieve to figure out what I'm going to

say to him. Stripping out of my gear, I drop it into my locker and then step into a pair of shorts and a Knights T-shirt.

I spare a quick glance at Noah as I'm walking out the door. His eyes are locked on mine. Noah's face is unreadable. Fuck. I hope he's still around when I'm done.

"Graham. That was a great game tonight," the reporter from the Nashville Star who travels with the team tells me. "How did that big play develop?"

I shake my head, a smile spreading across my face.

Hockey. This is easy. I can talk about hockey. "This is what we practice for. Knowing what to look for so you can stop the play in its tracks. Luckily I was there and was able to get the puck when we needed it to stop Colorado from scoring."

"Did it feel good to beat the reigning champions?"

"Felt awesome."

"Do you think it helped having Noah Fields in the stands tonight?"

That gets a small smile out of me. "We definitely didn't want to disappoint him. Even though he's out, we want to keep playing hard. Make a push for the playoffs."

"It would be the first time the Knights have made the playoffs in over a decade."

"I'm trying not to think about that," I tell them honestly. "I just want to do what I can to contribute to the Knights and help us win games."

"Thanks, Graham."

"Thank you."

Heading back toward the locker room, I pull open the door and crash into someone.

Someone that is *very* familiar to me.

Noah.

"Hey."

"Hi." God, up close he looks even better. His brown eyes are clear. "How are you feeling?"

Noah nods, rubbing a hand down the back of his neck. "Good. Shoulder still hurts every now and then, but good. I'm glad to finally be out of the sling."

I nod. "And your head? It's okay?"

"About the same as my shoulder. Still getting some headaches, but not nearly as bad."

"That's great to hear."

I breathe a sigh of relief. Even though I knew how he was doing—secondhand from my parents—it's better to hear it from him. To see him feels even better.

"I should get going."

"Wait."

I don't think. For once in my life, I don't weigh every decision and just do what I'm feeling. I grab Noah's hand and pull him toward me. His eyes go wide as his front slams into me.

I don't know where he was headed, but I don't care. I don't want him to leave.

Because if he does, I don't know if I'll have the balls to do this again.

His eyes widen as he looks me directly in the eye. "What are you doing?"

"What I was too scared to do before."

I kiss him. I pour every ounce of feeling I've had since he left Nashville into this kiss. Sadness. Anger. Frustration. Love.

I shut my brain off and give in to what I want.

Noah Fields.

"Wait." Noah pulls back, an unreadable look on his face. "I thought you didn't want to be out."

"I didn't. I was scared. I still am because I have no idea

if this is what you want anymore. If *I'm* what you want. Because I'm damn well afraid I ruined everything."

"Are you sure though? I don't want you to do this because you feel pressured," Noah tells me.

"Are you trying to talk me out of this?"

That has a hint of a smile tugging at the corner of Noah's mouth. "Considering you just kissed me in a locker room full of reporters, I'd say I really can't."

My eyes widen as I stop to take in the room around us. There's not much by way of privacy in here. The locker room has gone silent. I've never heard a group of guys be so quiet.

And every eye is locked on the two of us.

Including the reporters that are here covering the team. The only sound in the locker room is the clicks of their cameras.

"Shit." I scrub a hand down my face. "I guess I really didn't think this through."

"Hey. You don't have to be scared alone."

"No?"

A smile stretches across Noah's face. "I can hold your hand through it."

My smile matches his. "That's all I want."

Because it means I get to be with the one guy I well and truly want. The soft look on Noah's face has me further confessing to him.

"I love you, Noah. And I hate that it took you getting injured to make me realize it, but if it got us here…"

"I love you too," Noah cuts me off. "Now, go change so we can go out and get drinks. Piper is buying."

"Did I miss something?" I laugh.

Fuck. It's been awhile since I've done that and it feels good. Really damn good.

"Yeah. She bet against the Knights."

I shake my head. "Never bet against us."

"I can say the same about you and me."

I lick my lips, giving Noah one last kiss. Now that I can, I don't think I'll ever stop. "I'll take that bet every day of the week."

Chapter Twenty-Nine

NOAH

"How long has this been going on?" Jasper asks from across the table.

"Officially?" Graham checks the time on his phone before leaning back in his chair. "An hour or so?"

Nick rolls his eyes at us. "Seriously. How long?"

I shrug a shoulder, grabbing Graham's glass and taking a small sip. I don't want to be drinking, but if this is how the evening is going to go, I need at least one sip.

"A few months?"

I peer over at him. The smile on Graham's mouth lights up his entire face. I love that I put it there. That it's not one of pain.

It's one that I'm going to strive to put on his face every day for the rest of our lives.

"A few months," Graham confirms.

Marcus eyes the two of us from across the table. "I don't know how we missed this. It seems so obvious now."

Bode lets out a laugh, one that is a full-on cackle. "Dude. Were you two trying to bone the night we invaded your room?"

Graham winces. "I wouldn't call it that, but yes. You guys really are a bunch of cock-blockers."

Marcus smacks Bode on the back of the head. "Really? I'm surprised any woman falls for your charm."

He flashes a wide, cocky grin at him. "What can I say? I'm a charmer."

I snort a laugh. "I don't think that's what we call you, but okay."

"I don't know if I like having you back."

"Hey, none of that talk," Graham interjects. "He'll be kicking your ass next year on the ice."

Dax rolls his eyes at him. "You know you don't need to do that to your own teammate, right?"

Bode laughs at him. "Kinda like how these two started?" He waggles a finger between me and Graham.

"Maybe Graham was trying to hide his real feelings toward you," Jasper tells us.

Graham shakes his head, draping his arm over the back of my chair. "No. I really didn't like him."

"And now you love me. Who would have thought?"

I lean over and take a kiss from him. I don't have to hide anymore. Not that I ever did, but I don't have to hide what this man means to me.

"Who would have thought?" Graham whispers against my lips as he pulls back.

I don't think I've ever seen Graham look so happy, but I'm pretty sure I look the same way.

The guys start rehashing the game from earlier tonight, leaving Graham and me to ourselves.

"I wish we didn't have to leave first thing tomorrow for Edmonton." Graham drops his elbow on the table and shifts so I'm the sole focus of his attention.

"Will it make you feel better if I'm waiting for you when you get home?"

"Yeah?"

I nod, moving so my knees are between his, dropping my hands there. "Yeah. I mean, I can do my rehab from anywhere. Might as well be close to you."

"That sounds amazing."

I hold my hand out to Graham and he takes it without thinking. "I have to admit. Part of coming back here was because I was running away."

"I'm sorry."

I shake my head at Graham's words. "No. It's okay. You weren't ready and I knew the score when we started this thing. So it was easier to run back here."

Graham squeezes my hand. "No more running, okay? I promise, I won't either."

"No running. Ever." Cupping his cheek, I pull Graham toward me and seal our words with a kiss. It feels damn good to be here with my boyfriend. To not care that anyone in this bar can see us.

"God. You two are disgustingly in love."

Bode's words pull us apart. That fucker.

"Leave them alone." Jasper smacks him on the back of the head.

"I'm going to go find someone that I don't have to be in love with tonight." Bode laughs, heading toward the bar where a group of women are standing.

"Seriously. He needs to keep it in his pants. I'm surprised it hasn't fallen off." Marcus is shaking his head at him.

"And on that note, I'm heading back to the hotel. I'm wiped." Dax drops his empty glass on the table in front of him. "It was good seeing you, Strawberry."

"I'll go with you." Marcus drains the last of his drink.

"Yeah. You too." I give Dax a quick hug as he and Marcus head out. "See you back in Nashville."

"Hold up. I don't want to be left with these two." Jasper gives us a quick wave and follows the guys out.

It's just the two of us.

Well, the two of us and our families and the guys from the Black Diamonds. They've been at their own tables just to the right of us.

Our group is taking up the majority of the back room of the bar. It's weird to see so many people I love back here.

My dad and his friends.

The guys from my old team.

The guys from my new team.

Graham.

He is the most important person here.

Everything about this night has been damn near perfect.

"What's this I hear about you heading back to Nashville?" Mom asks.

My mom and Frankie take the now vacated seats across from us, with Piper taking the empty one beside me.

"It's about damn time." Piper laughs. "I don't need to be losing any more bets."

"You bet your brother?" Graham asks.

Piper nods. "That the Black Diamonds would win."

"Ouch. I don't feel bad for you buying the drinks then."

Piper waves him off. "Yeah, yeah. I guess it was a good win."

"I feel betrayed." Cash pops up next to her. "See if I get you another drink."

He walks off to the bar and Piper follows him, a big smile on her face.

"Do you think they know they're ignoring our question?" Frankie asks.

"Mom. Really?" Graham groans.

I snort a laugh. Having been around each other for so many years, it seems like our parents have merged into one person. They all are always thinking the same thing, it seems.

The best ways to fuss over their children.

"So you are going home to Nashville?" Mom asks.

Home. That word sounds so good. Looking at Graham, I answer, "Yeah, I am."

"Are you going to take care of him, Graham? Make sure he follows his PT regimen? We don't have Piper to make sure he stays on track."

"Mommmm," I groan. "Can you not? I'm over thirty years old."

"I don't want you to be too in love and doing what you do and forget to take care of yourself."

"Kill. Me. Now," I mutter, dropping my head onto Graham's shoulder.

I guess it doesn't matter how old you are, your parents will always embarrass you.

Graham ignores me though, wrapping an arm around my waist. "I promise. I will make sure to take care of him."

Mom's eyes are watering. "I just want to make sure my baby is taken care of."

"Tenley." Dad comes up behind her and pulls her into his hold. "Noah is a grown-up and can take care of himself."

She smacks him. "I'll always worry about my baby."

"If Graham doesn't, I'll make sure to come out and kick his ass." Frankie now enters the conversation, much to Graham's dismay.

"I'm suddenly becoming more and more grateful at how far Nashville is from Denver." I laugh.

I love our families. I do. But I want to be with Graham.

In Nashville without someone watching over me. It's been a long month.

I'm finally on the road to feeling better. And that's what I want to focus on.

There's no longer this sadness clouding my head. I'm no longer worrying about my future with the team.

Everything feels bright.

With Graham by my side, I can't wait to see what comes next.

Chapter Thirty

NOAH - TWO MONTHS LATER

"This sucks," I grumble. Looking around the locker room, trash bins sit in front of lockers as guys clean out their stalls.

"Hey. We'll get there next year," Graham tells me, grabbing a stick of deodorant and tossing it into his bag. "I know we will."

We were one game away from making it to the playoffs. It would have been the first time in ten years that the Knights made it. With a few well-timed wins, it was looking good. Until an overtime goal by Vancouver knocked us out of the running.

The loss stings even more when I couldn't contribute to the team. Not that anyone blames me since I was put on IR, but it still hurts.

It really fucking hurts.

"Hey, don't jinx us."

"You've already won a few cups," Graham points out to me, dropping down onto the bench to zip up his bag. With my locker clean, I wandered over here to help him.

Not that he needs it. I just want to be near him.

The press portion of the day is already over. It's never fun talking to them about how we're out of it and what we can do to improve for next year. They fired more questions at me about my game and if I'll be back than anything else.

I can only tell them what I hope to be true—that I'll be back in top form and ready to go. I'm feeling good—no, great—and am ready to get back to training.

"Yeah, but I haven't won one with you."

Now that we have each other, it's one of the only things I can think of doing. Winning one with Graham. Hoisting that trophy over our heads as we kiss one another.

Yeah, I want it. *Bad.*

"You're such a sap." Graham leans over and presses his lips against mine. I love being with him like this. Not having to worry about who might see us or who might judge Graham for being with me.

The guys in here don't care. Even though we've been together for months, it still feels new. We've been out together a few times, but no one seems to pay us any attention.

Graham adapted faster than I thought he would. I'm lucky. Because I love being with him like this. Being with him is easy. The best thing to ever happen to me.

"I can't help it when it comes to you." I squeeze his leg.

Marcus comes over to us, slinging his bag across his shoulders. "I've got a few hours before I need to be home. Want to grab a drink with a few of the guys?"

Graham and I glance at one another. "Sure."

"If you two can peel yourselves off each other."

"Just because you're not dating anyone, asshole," Graham chirps.

A hard look comes over Marcus's face before he stalks out toward the parking lot.

"Wonder what that's about," I ask him.

"Beats the hell out of me."

"If it's not about the girls, I don't know what it could be."

Graham shrugs. "Well, let's not keep him waiting. I want some drinks and then I want to get home and start our offseason."

"You and I have a very different idea on how this offseason is going to go."

Graham stands, holding his hand out to me, his box of shit from his locker tucked under his other arm. I can't help the smile on my face at how openly affectionate Graham is. I love it. I love not having to hide our relationship. "Oh, I know exactly how I want it to go."

"You realize buying a house means we actually have to move shit in and not relax?"

Graham groans as the two of us head out, hand in hand. "What if I don't want to?"

"You bought it."

"Correction. We're *buying* it. I want something that is just ours. Sue me."

It has a big grin washing over my face. "Ours. I like the sound of that."

"No more tiny condo."

Pushing open the door to the arena, the bright Nashville sun greets us. A few of the guys are already pulling out as the two of us head to my truck.

"It was better than that crappy hotel of yours."

I wince. "You never even saw it, so you can't complain."

"Doesn't matter. We're both getting an upgrade."

Opening the door to the truck, we drop our bags in the backseat before climbing in the front.

"Are you sure it's not too late to hire movers?" I ask.

"We're not hiring movers. Besides, we don't even have a place yet. We might not even find anything until next season."

With our season ending sooner than we liked, we hadn't planned on starting the house hunt this soon. We know where we want to live, but we just need to find something. We're not in any kind of hurry.

"I did find a few places." I hold out my hand for Graham to take while steering us toward the bar with the other.

"Send them to me. We can look tonight."

I laugh. "Our first night of the offseason and this is how we're going to spend it?"

"Oh. It's only part of it. I plan on spending the rest of it with you buried in my ass."

"I fucking hate you. How am I supposed to make it through drinks with my dick at half-mast?"

"Only half-mast?" Graham reaches over, giving me a pat on my thickening erection. "I must be losing my touch."

"Seriously. I hate you, Graham."

"I love you too, Noah."

I scoff, a smile giving me away. "Yeah, yeah."

"ALRIGHT, WHAT ARE WE CHEERSING TO?" I ask.

The bar isn't crowded for this early in the afternoon. It's a dive bar, a few blocks away from the rink, but for some reason, it's never overrun with fans. Makes it perfect for us when we want to hang out but not be in the public eye.

The old, dark-paneled walls make it darker in here

than it is outside. Country music plays on the jukebox in the front of the bar. The owner, a Knights fan, keeps a corner of the bar reserved for us. With a wall blocking the booths back here, it makes it the perfect spot for us.

"Well, not the playoffs," Marcus says, tongue-in-cheek.

"Offseason?" I ask.

"A new house?" Graham says.

"Where are you guys moving?" Dax asks.

"We're looking at buying," I tell them. "We wanted our own place together."

"Aww. Don't want the single life of Nashville anymore?" Bode teases.

"Fucker." Graham flips him off.

"Leave them alone," Jasper butts in. "Let them have their peace."

"God, you really are getting old, Jas," Marcus tells him. "Can we fucking toast now? I don't have all day and my arm is getting tired."

"Fine. To the Knights," I say as we all clink our glasses together.

"To the Knights!" everyone echoes.

The guys are chattering about anything and everything. This is just how things were back home. It's what I love most about being on a team.

Leaning back in my chair as the next round of drinks are poured, a happiness I haven't felt in a long time spreads through me.

When I got traded, I thought that it would be the end of everything good. That my relationships at home would be strained with me being so far away. That the only reason I had the friendships back home that I did was because we played together.

It's so far from the truth, I could laugh.

I found a new family here. I found Graham.

I found everything.

"What's got you so happy?" Graham asks.

"This. You. The guys."

"Really?"

I nod, sipping on my beer. "If you had told me a year ago that I would be in this place right now, I wouldn't have believed you. I was a touch bitter when I first came here."

Graham winces. "I didn't exactly make it easy for you."

"You? Never," Bode interrupts. "I thought you two were going to kill each other."

"Hey! We would not have," I argue.

Marcus snorts a laugh. "You mean before or after the time you two got into a fight?"

"Really. You two hated each other," Jasper agrees.

"More than I hate my own brother," Dax tells us.

"Your brother is a shithead and I will die on that hill," I point out. "Sorry, but when he cheats on my sister, there is no coming back from that."

The fucker. Duncan played for the Black Diamonds, cheated on Piper, and then was cut because he was sleeping with the assistant coach's wife.

Real stand-up guy. Thankfully Dax is nothing like him.

Dax sighs. A long-suffering sigh that says it's not the first time he's had this conversation. Nor is it one that he wants to be having.

"Don't worry. I hate him for it too. Among other things."

"What—"

"Drop it," Graham whispers to me, ending the conversation.

"Alright boys. I have to get going." Marcus stands, dropping a few bills on the table. "Drink responsibly, please. If any of you need to be bailed out of jail, don't call me, Bode."

Everyone bursts out laughing as the man in question flips him off. "Fuck off."

"Like I said, be responsible."

A few more guys come and go as the drinks start to go down easier. Graham doesn't have more than one, so as the bar gets more crowded as the night goes on, we decide to leave and walk home.

The night air is cool as dozens of people head toward downtown to party.

"You know. We could always go find our own party." I snicker, grabbing Graham's ass as we turn up the road that we live on.

Graham wraps an arm around my waist and tugs me close. "The only party we're going to have is at home in bed."

"Fucking finally!" I shout, a little too loud.

"What? Can't keep it in your pants, Fields?"

"More like you tormenting me all night."

Graham laughs as our building comes into view. "You know you love it when I edge you."

Slapping his ass, I hurry us off toward the elevator. As soon as it arrives, I'm on him. Kissing him. Licking his neck. Holding him like I'll never have to let him go.

"Now who's edging who?" Graham asks.

A dirty smile spreads across my face. "Suck me off and then I'll fuck you?"

Graham returns the smile, pulling me tight to him.

"Best of both worlds, baby."

Epilogue

"**H**ow did you two manage to collect this much stuff?" Uncle Knox grumbles, setting another one of the many boxes down in the living room.

"Getting old there, Knoxy?" Uncle Colin asks, dropping a box on the coffee table. "Can't handle a few boxes?"

"Fuck you. Not all of us rolled in late to help."

"I wasn't late!" Colin fires back.

"You weren't here with the rest of us."

"Someone had to bring breakfast."

The two of them delve into an argument that we've all heard before.

"Do you think they do this because they don't know how much they really love each other?" Graham whispers, handing me a beer in our new kitchen.

"Oh, definitely."

It's been like this for as long as I can remember. Uncle Knox and Uncle Colin bickering. I can't help but smile as our families help us move into our new place.

When we told them about moving into a house

together—a place of our own—they descended upon us to help us move.

We found a recently renovated older home in a gated community on the outskirts of Nashville. Something quiet. Away from the craziness of downtown.

Breathing room for the two of us to grow together.

With all the furniture having been delivered yesterday, it's starting to feel like a real home. The large windows face the sprawling backyard, letting in the afternoon sun.

The perfect space for us.

"How many more boxes?" Bode whines, dropping another one onto the kitchen counter.

"Only a few," Marcus tells him.

Bode points at me, a tired look on his face. "You're buying drinks the next time we're out."

"The least I can do." I tip my head at him in acknowledgment.

"Could have hired movers," he mutters under his breath as Nick walks into the kitchen.

"What has you two so happy?" Nick grabs a beer from the fridge before settling onto a barstool at the large, white marble island.

"Can't we be happy?" I fire back, wrapping an arm around Graham's waist. The face he gives me has me wanting to kick everyone out and break in our new bedroom.

"It's nice to see, that's all." Nick holds his bottle out for a cheers.

"Speaking of happy. No Bex this week?" I ask.

A dopey grin washes over his face. "Nah. She has a meeting in New York this week."

"You going to meet up with her there?" Noah asks, leaning across the counter.

"Planning on it. You two planning on doing anything with the rest of your offseason?"

Graham scoffs. "Other than moving in? No."

"Hey. We have some plans."

"Like?" Graham sips his beer.

A devious smile crosses my face. One that is a promise of things to come.

"Things I can't say in mixed company."

The doorbell rings, signifying the pizza we ordered is here.

"I'll get that. I don't want to hear about your sex life." Nick runs out of the kitchen to the front door.

"Soooo…what I'm hearing is if we start talking about sex, we'll scare everyone out?" Graham asks, rubbing his hand up and down my back. "Think it'll work?"

"Fat chance, boys." Uncle Alex walks into the kitchen with half the pizza boxes while Uncle Carter is behind him. "There is no scaring us off."

"Damn," I mutter under my breath. "Then everyone better hurry up and eat."

"Is that any way to talk to the people who moved you into your house?" Dad claps me on the shoulder.

"If it gets you out of here faster, yes."

Troy pops open the lid of one of the boxes and grabs a slice. "I'm only in town a few days, and you're trying to get rid of me? Rude."

"I don't feel bad at all," Graham fires back.

"Well, we're not even close to being done," Frankie tells us, worming her way between Graham and me. "We have to make this house a home."

"It is, Mom," Graham tells her, groaning.

It's a feeling I know well. Of mothers smothering us.

We might have a long way to go in settling in, but the

fact that this is our own place—together—means everything.

We're not just roommates anymore. We're partners. In hockey. In life. In everything.

I never thought that this is where the two of us would end up.

It's the only place I want to be.

"Oh no. These walls are too white," Mom reiterates. "We need to get some paint up here. Maybe some pictures."

"I agree. Maybe gray? Or a navy? We'll have to see what the light looks like in the afternoon."

"While you're planning, maybe put a big ol' picture of me up in the living room. It'd look great." Uncle Colin throws an arm around both of our shoulders, sandwiching Frankie in between us.

"Great idea," Knox tells him. "We can use it as a dartboard."

"Stop it, you two," Frankie tells him as Knox flips Colin off.

Dad rolls his eyes at him as he comes into the kitchen. "The house looks good as it is in case they don't get to it, Ten."

"I'm just saying it could use a little love." She ignores Dad as he presses a kiss to her head.

"We'll be fine, Mom."

She ignores us, talking with Frankie. "I've got some time before the school year starts. I need to make sure everything is all set here before heading home."

"I agree. Offseason training doesn't start for a few weeks," Frankie confirms. "The two of us can knock it out in a week, I think."

"Or we can hire someone," Graham tells them, but they wave us off.

"It's a lost cause. Just let them be," I tell him, pressing a kiss to his cheek.

Heading to the fridge, I grab a fresh beer for myself and lean back against the counter, taking in this group of people.

When I got traded to Nashville, this was the very last place I thought I would end up. I thought I would be on an island of one playing out the last few years of my career before moving back to Denver.

To the only home I've ever known.

Now? Now this ranch house on the outskirts of Nashville is the only one I can imagine. Moving in with Graham? It was so far off my radar, I would have laughed if you told me.

But it's the only place I want to be. Here, in our home with the family the two of us have amassed. Our *real* family and our found families through hockey.

"Hey." Graham walks over, wrapping his arms around me. He slots perfectly against me—like he was made for me and me alone. "You okay?"

"Perfect. Couldn't be any better."

Graham presses a warm kiss to my lips, and I hate that the noise of the kitchen rings heavy in my ears. Now I really wish that everyone was gone.

Because I want to have my way with this man in every room of our home.

"It can wait." Graham pulls back, whispering in my ear.

"Think you can read my mind?" I quirk a brow at him, draping an arm around his shoulders and pulling him close.

"Yes." He nods. "I know exactly what you're thinking. Trust me, I want it too."

"We should probably eat if we're going to have any energy to finish unpacking today."

"Ugh. You're right." Graham drops his head into my neck before spinning around to face the crowd that's gathered around the island.

Paper plates are filled with greasy triangles of pizza as the conversation starts to filter into my brain.

"And to think, if I had a kid, he could've ended up with Graham," Colin tells Dad.

"What in the world are you talking about?" Knox sighs.

"I'm just saying. If Peyton and I had kids, Graham would've been lucky to end up with them."

"No way. Not on my watch," Graham interjects.

Colin throws up his hands. "It was hypothetical."

"I'll take on your kid."

"Again, hypothetical." Colin glances toward Knox. "Tell him."

"Oh no. You got yourself into this mess. You can get out of it."

"Is it always like this?" Marcus asks. As the new guy, he hasn't been around all of us together to know what they're like.

Before I can answer, Mom is interrupting their conversation. "I swear, the older you all get, the more like teenagers you act."

"Is this what we have to look forward to?" Nick asks.

Carter shakes his head at my best friend and his only son. "No. You're too mature for these guys, even at your age."

"Hey!" Knox and Colin shout at the same time.

"What? He's telling the truth," Alex tells them.

And just like that, the rest of them dive into another

argument about who is the most mature of them in the room.

Even if I want to kick them out, I wouldn't have it any other way.

BY THE TIME EVERYONE LEAVES, heading back to their respective places, Graham and I are collapsing onto our bed.

"I'm too tired to move."

"Every bone in my body hurts. Worse than playing hockey," Graham bemoans. "We should have hired somebody."

"I don't want strangers in our house."

"I like the sound of that." Graham turns his head to me.

"What?"

"Our house."

Smiling at him, I press my lips to his. Savoring the taste of him. That the two of us are here together in this moment.

"Think it's time to christen this place?"

I slide my hand under the waistband of his shorts, feeling the muscles of his ass grow taut.

"I love you, Noah, but I am too tired."

That has me popping up onto my elbow and looking down at the man with his eyes closed. "Really? Not even a quick blow job?"

Graham quirks one eye open before closing it. "Think you could even get it up, old man?"

I slap his ass. "The one I'm worried about is you here. I'm perfectly fine."

Graham rolls over onto his back, resting one arm behind his head.

The only thing in our room is our bed and a nightstand. All of the boxes that go in here will be dealt with tomorrow. Our main concern was unpacking the rest of the house.

The two of us can take care of in here.

"You know we'll have the rest of our lives to do whatever we want here, right?"

I groan, snuggling into his warm side. "So sue me; I want to have a fun night on the *very first night* in our own house with my boyfriend."

Turning on his side, Graham pins me with a stare that tells me I'm going to like whatever he says next. "How about hand jobs? That's about all I can muster the energy for. Then tomorrow—"

"Tomorrow what?"

I'm already moving in closer, tracing kisses along his unshaven jaw. Letting the bristles rub against my soft lips as I tug his earlobe between my teeth.

Graham cups my growing erection through my shorts.

"Tomorrow I will let you fuck me in every room of this house. Sound good?"

I give him a cocky grin before taking my time kissing him. Getting lost in the taste of him. The feel of him.

"So what you're saying is it's the best of both worlds?"

"Yeah. Best of both worlds."

"Then I'll say yes to anything you ever want. As long as it's you and me."

Graham's answering kiss is all I'll ever need.

Moving to Nashville from Denver gave me everything I was looking for in life when I thought it would be the end of everything.

Denver and Nashville.

Hockey and Graham.

It really is the best of both worlds.

THE END

Keep reading for a bonus scene with Noah and Graham...

Bonus Scene

NOAH - A FEW YEARS LATER

"You really want to retire?" Graham asks me one more time. "You're sure?"

I nod, sipping on my beer. Darkness has fallen all around us. String lights hang above us on our patio as lightning bugs flicker and crickets chirp in our backyard.

I let out a peaceful sigh. "I'm positive. What else do I need to achieve in my career that I haven't already?"

"It's going to be weird playing without you," Graham tells me, his feet tangling with mine on our outdoor lounger.

"You've played without me before," I tell him.

"Yeah, but I like playing with you better."

"Aww. You really do love me."

Throwing an arm around Graham, I pull him close and press a kiss to the top of his head.

"Considering we've been living together for however long it's been now, I think that's obvious." Graham's laugh vibrates through me.

"Just think though. I'll be here waiting for you when you get home from your away games."

"I'll be a kept man. Even if I'll miss bunking with you on the road."

I laugh. "I don't think I'll miss those long road stretches. Even if I'll miss you."

"As long as you're here when I get home."

"There's no other place in the world I'd be."

I take a deep breath of the warm, spring air. Even though this season didn't end how we wanted it to, I'm okay with it.

Because I've accomplished more in my career than many could even hope to dream about. Especially these last few years with the Knights.

I never thought I'd get back to my prime like I was with the Black Diamonds, but I did. And it helped establish the Knights as one of the league's premier teams. We're no longer a joke. The team that no longer is circled by others as a guaranteed win.

I love that I helped with that. But I'm too old to keep playing. I can't keep up with the younger guys, and I want to be able to enjoy life after hockey. It's to the point where my body just isn't there anymore.

And I'm okay with that.

Nights like this with the man I love are what I want now. Not chasing another cup or another win.

"Besides, if I really want to, I can travel to any of your away games that I want."

Graham barks out a laugh this time, deep and hearty. "You were already traveling to all the games when you played."

"Hey." I elbow him in the side. "See if I come to any of your home games now either."

Graham presses a cool kiss to my cheek. "I know you'll be there. Rocking my jersey now. I couldn't keep you away even if I tried."

"No, you couldn't. I'll be the most obnoxious person in the stands."

Graham groans. "Oh god, you will be, won't you?"

I nod, smiling to myself. "Calling out the refs and yelling at the opposing team. It'll be perfect."

"Do you think it'll be hard?" Graham asks, setting down his empty beer bottle on the table in front of us.

I shrug a shoulder. "At first, yes. It'll be weird not having hockey, but I'll get used to it. Find something else to do so I'm not twiddling my thumbs everyday."

"You know…" Graham starts.

"What?"

"Since neither of us have anything to do tomorrow…" Graham shifts, throwing one knee over my lap, straddling me.

"Have something in mind?"

Having my sexy as hell boyfriend leaning over me is something I don't think I'll ever get over.

Graham leans over me, tugging my earlobe between his teeth. "If I have to tell you, I don't think I'm doing it right."

"Then why don't you show me."

Graham pulls back and gives me a wicked smile. "How about a celebratory blow job for retirement?"

"Mmm." I'm practically purring and I don't even care. "I wonder how often I could use this excuse to get a blow job from you."

Graham gets down on his knees for me and grabs the beer bottle from my hand. He swigs back the last few sips before setting it on the table behind him. "Giving you a blow job? You only have to ask."

Grabbing the hem of my shorts, Graham pulls them down my legs and tosses them over his shoulder. Seeing as how I changed when we got home after locker clean out, I didn't put anything else on besides them. My cock is already hard and leaking at the attention from Graham.

His strong hands move up my thighs, brushing lightly against my balls. While his attention is solely on my dick, he doesn't give me the relief I'm seeking.

A quick squeeze here. Another brush there. Graham is edging me as my precum starts to leak from the head of my cock.

"What the fuck are you waiting for?" I growl. "Can't you see I'm ready?"

"You know." Graham rests his elbow on the lounger next to me and stares into my eyes. Big brown eyes that are full of love and playfulness. The fucker. "You're awfully demanding now that you're retired. You're not the captain anymore which means you're not the boss of me."

"Fuck me." I throw my head back in pain. I'm ready to explode and all I want is Graham's mouth on me when I do.

"I believe that's your job." At those words, Graham swallows me down to the base.

"Oh fuck." The relief is immediate. There is nothing better than Graham's mouth on me. Well, except maybe being buried inside of him. But that will come later.

Pushing my fingers through his hair, I slow his movements. His mouth looks perfect wrapped around me as his free hands plays with my balls.

"So fucking good," I whisper. "God, your mouth."

Graham smiles as best he can around me, but doesn't pop off. With each suck, I'm that much closer to exploding down his throat.

My balls start to seize up as fire moves through me. With one final squeeze, I erupt. Pouring everything I have down his throat as Graham swallows every last drop.

"Fuck!" I shout into the quiet night. My hips lift off the

cushions and push down Graham's throat as he takes everything I give him. "Yes, yes, yes!"

As I float back down to Earth, my entire body is boneless.

Graham wipes his mouth as he takes a seat beside me and pulls me into his arms. "Since you're retired now…"

"Yes?" I ask, looking up at him. His own dick is hard as granite, poking me in the side.

"I think you'll have more energy to fuck me now."

This time, it's me who's moving so I'm on top of him. Cupping his dick through his shorts, I give it a hard squeeze. "What are you saying?"

"I think that means you'll have more than enough energy to fuck me every time I come home from a long road trip."

"Or any game really."

"True."

I nod, squeezing him harder. "Or every night."

Graham smiles, his eyes filled with nothing but lust. "Whenever we want."

I smile back at him, taking his lips in a sweet kiss. "We have all the time in the world."

Want more bi-awakening? Then check out Merry in Moose Falls!

Want a bonus scene with Noah and Graham? Grab it now!

And make sure to preorder the Nashville Knights! Book one, Game Misconduct, is coming February 28, 2025.

Acknowledgments

Book 22 is out in the world!

And with it, we're closing the chapter on the Black Diamonds** and entering the next chapter…the Nashville Knights! We are firmly in our hockey era and I am here for it!

I am so happy to finally have Noah and Graham's story out in the world — I had so many readers message me asking for their story and I hope you love them as much as I do.

Thank you to my beta readers Trish and Menctah for helping me with this story. To Tina for being one of my favorite people in the world…I love you bunches! To all of my author friends that I am lucky to know…Lily, Claire, Swati, Maria…I love you all! To my street team and reader group — thank you for sharing and loving my stories.

To all the readers who have taken a chance on my books and share the love — THANK YOU! I love getting to talk to you and share our love of books. This is truly the best job in the world…all because of you.

<3 Emily

**Are we though?? Stay tuned…

Also by Emily Silver

Colorado Black Diamonds Hockey

Best Kept Secret

Best Laid Plans

Best of the Best

Best of Both Worlds

Nashville Knights

Game Misconduct - Marcus and Harper's story, coming February 2025

Dixon Creek Ranch

Yours to Take

Yours to Hold

Yours to Be

Yours to Forget

Yours To Lose

Yours To Love - a newsletter freebie

The Denver Mountain Lions

Roughing The Kicker

Pass Interference

Sideline Infraction

Illegal Contact

The Big Game

Standalones

Off the Deep End

The Highland Escape

Power Pose

Merry in Moose Falls

Love Pucked - a sapphic hockey romance, coming early 2025

The Ainsworth Royals

Royal Reckoning

Reckless Royal

Royal Relations

Royal Roots

The Love Abroad Series

An Icy Infatuation

A French Fling

A Sydney Surprise

Scan the QR code to read my books now!

About the Author

After winning a Young Author's Award in second grade, Emily Silver was destined to be a writer. She loves writing inclusive stories, with strong heroines and the swoony men who fall for them.

A lover of all things romance, Emily started writing books set in her favorite places around the world. As an avid traveler, she's been to all seven continents and sailed around the globe.

When she's not writing, Emily can be found sipping cocktails on her porch, reading all the romance she can get her hands on and planning her next big adventure!

Find her on social media to stay up to date on all her adventures and upcoming releases!